# EVERY
# BOSS
## HAS A
## Soft Spot

A NOVEL BY

# DANIELLE MAY

# ACKNOWLEDGEMENTS & DEDICATION

First, I would like to give glory to God for presenting me with such an incredible opportunity. I would have never thought of having a career as an author, but you had it in your will. Thank you for giving me an amazing gift as well as allowing me to discover it. Whenever I'm doubting myself, I have a talk with you, and you come through for me each time, giving me the strength to move forward.

To my friends, it's so much that I can say about y'all, but I want to give a special thanks to Ashley. There have been times where I wanted to stop because I compared myself to other authors, but it was you who encouraged me to keep doing what I was doing and to always stay true to who I was. Thank you for being the realest friend that I have.

To the readers, thank you for giving me a chance. I appreciate everyone that took the time out of their lives just to read it. That means so much to me. I will continue to put out content that will hopefully keep you guys entertained and wanting more. Thank you so much. Be on the lookout for part two! It'll be out shortly.

CONTACT ME:

*Facebook: Danielle May*

*Email: Labryar93@gmail.com*

*Snapchat: labryar93*

# Sasha

"What the fuck you getting mad for? I told you I didn't do shit with that girl. You better calm yo' ass down before I yoke yo' ass up!" my boyfriend, Kendrick, shouted, getting up from his position on the couch as he made his way toward me, wearing an angry scowl.

I couldn't help but shake my head at his dumb ass. We had been going through the same thing for the past couple of months. Every time I confronted him about his cheating ways, he would deny what he did, blow up, and then throw out some tired ass threat, and honestly, I was tired of going back and forth with him over the same thing. I had other things to worry about, and after today, his ass would no longer be one of them.

"I must've been imagining shit when I saw you tonguing down that girl in the mall, right? She was choking, and you helped her by preforming mouth-to-mouth resuscitation on her while grabbing her ass, huh?" I asked sarcastically, crossing my arms over my chest, ready to hear what lie he would come up with.

He looked at me for a minute before backing up, chuckling to himself. "You know what? Fuck this. I have other shit to do besides deal with yo' insecure ass right now. I'll holla at you when you're not so damn emotional." He walked out the front door of my apartment.

Following behind him, I caught the door before it could shut. "You don't have to ever worry about bringing your ass back over here. I'm done with yo' trifling ass!" I called out, slamming the door.

Heading straight to my bedroom, I closed the door before lying across my bed, shedding silent tears. Even though I suspected Kendrick was cheating on me for a while, I never really had proof, only hearing a couple of people that I associated with telling me they saw him out with different girls. I confronted him about it multiple times, but without actual evidence, I couldn't really say anything until I saw him kissing on a girl in the middle of the mall today. I wasn't going to lie; it did hurt me, seeing that. We were together for three years. I met him during my sophomore year of college in speech class, and we instantly clicked. He was funny, always making me laugh, and the fact that he was hella cute to me didn't hurt either. But over the last year, it was like he changed into a different person. He no longer was the person that I had fallen for. Was I hurting right now? Of course. Would I get over it? In time, yes, but I knew one thing, though. There was no way we could ever be together again. Once a person cheated on me, there was no going back.

This wasn't where I saw myself being at the age of twenty-three. Ever since I was younger, I always had dreams of becoming a well-known name in the painters and art community with my painting being in several museums. I wanted to travel to different countries so that I could showcase my pieces and have people experience all different types of emotions once they laid eyes on them. But I guess the saying was true: if you want to make God laugh, tell him your plans for your life. For as long as I could remember, I loved painting. I felt like it was the only way I could express myself without using words. Once I started painting, I entered a world that only I understood. I didn't have to worry about the judgment of the outside world or the pressures of society. Because here I was with a bachelor's degree in art, working at a call center that I hated; but until I found someone to invest in my painting, I was stuck.

Deciding to put all the emotions that I was feeling to good use, I got up from my bed to retrieve my painting tools that sat in the corner of the room. Then I started to paint, shutting out the outside world, pouring my heart into every line, shape, and color until I had nothing left to give.

Stepping back, I brushed my thick, bushy curls out of my face with the back of my hands before I looked over my masterpiece. A tiny smile crept on my lips as I admired what I had just drawn. It represented everything that I felt at the moment—sadness, confusion, hurt, loss, yet hopeful of a better tomorrow. *I was definitely hanging this up on the wall,* I thought to myself before hearing someone knocking at my door. I tried to ignore them, but the constant banging on the door was starting to get on my nerves. I set my tools down on my dresser, heading to the door to see who could possibly be knocking on my door like they didn't have any damn sense. As soon as I opened it, my cousin Tori burst through the door.

"What's up, bitch!" she yelled in an animated type of voice. I closed the door behind her.

"Do you have to be so damn loud all the time?" I asked, watching her go in my refrigerator like she lived here.

She turned around to look at me before she got one of my Red Bull drinks. "Eww, what's up with you and this funky ass attitude that you got? If I was anybody else, I would take offense to how you are talking to me and leave, but since I'm not, my ass is staying. Now let me guess, you and Kendrick had a fight again?"

Taking a seat on my couch, I looked at her as she did the same. I debated on if I wanted to have this conversation with her or not, but I was pretty sure I was going to tell her eventually anyways, so might as well do it now. "Yeah, I broke up with him after catching him boo'd up with some girl at the mall."

"What!" she shouted, nearly spitting out her drink. "I need more details than that."

Not caring to fully go into all the details, I gave her the short version. "I was at the mall to pick up some new candles from Bed, Bath & Beyond, and I ran into a girl named Jasmine that went to school with me. We made general conversation, then she asked me were Kendrick and I still together, and I told her we were. Before I could ask her why she asked me that, she grabbed my arm and literally pulled me to the food court. I was about to curse her out, but she pointed over toward a couple that was kissing, and imagine my surprise when I saw that it was Kendrick. Instead of showing my ass like I wanted to, I simply took a picture and waited for him to come over, then I broke it off."

"Damn, girl, I'm sorry you had to deal with his trifling ass, but I told you he wasn't no good when you first started dating his lame ass. I just felt like his ass was sneaky, but your love-sick ass didn't want to hear it."

I nodded my head in agreement. "I mean, it is what it is. I'll get over it. Maybe this was a sign that I needed to start really focusing on my future, you know?"

"Yeah, girl, I'm with you. Fuck these niggas and concentrate on being a brand. The only thing these niggas can do for you is get on your nerves and sling dick, and sometimes, it don't even be that good." She laughed while taking a sip of her drink.

"How you gon' say 'fuck niggas' when yo' ass is damn near married to Justin?" I questioned with a raised eyebrow, calling her out. Tori and Justin had been together since they were eighteen. Personally, I didn't know how they even managed to stay together as long as they did. My cousin was the definition of crazy, and Justin was ten times worse than she was, but who was I to judge their relationship? Both of them may have been crazy, but you could tell that they loved each other.

She frowned up her face. "My man is the exception. He knows not to pull that shit on me. He'll go to sleep with a dick and wake up with it lying right next to him in a jar," she said matter-of-factly, like it wasn't a crime. I honestly believed that she would do it, though. "So let me see what you painted," she said.

"What made you think that I painted something?"

"First off, you got on that ugly ass painting outfit you wear every time you paint, and since you dumped Kendrick, I know you wanted to go into that weird ass world of yours, and you only do that when you paint. You better stop acting like I don't know you like we didn't grow up together."

It was true. Tori was not only my cousin, but she was also my best friend and the one person that knew mostly everything about me. We both grew up in Georgia. We were thick as thieves; wherever you saw me, you saw her, and vice versa until my uncle's job relocated him to Houston, Texas, when Tori was sixteen. Even though we lived in different states, she used to spend every summer with me, and once I graduated, I end up moving to Texas with her, and we both attended University of Houston together. If you were on the outside looking in, you would wonder why we were so close because our personalities were so different from one another.

I was very laid-back, quiet, and preferred to be alone with my paintbrush, some paint, and a board. I didn't really talk to anyone or have people that I could call my friends. Most people didn't get me, and I didn't go out of my way to make them understand. On the other hand, there was Tori, who was very loud and outspoken. You never had to guess what was on her mind, because nine times out of ten, she would tell you. She didn't have a problem making friends, even though she had a hard time keeping them due to her blunt attitude. No one wanted to hear the truth all the time, but that's what you got when it came to her. She didn't sugarcoat anything.

I led her to what I called my painting room. I pointed to the painting I finished up a few minutes ago. I watched her look over it as I held my breath, waiting for her response. She was one of the only people whose opinion I actually valued.

"This is beautiful, Sasha. I mean, wow. You have a gift, baby girl. This has to be one of my favorites of your pieces. Do you mind if I post this to my Instagram and Snapchat?" she asked, already pulling out her phone to snap a picture.

"I don't care. It's probably the only exposure I will ever get, but I'm happy that you like it, though. Your opinion is very-much appreciated."

"Girl, please. You know you are going to make it, so don't even trip. Just keep doing what you are doing, and your hard work will pay off in due time. Ain't your mama always telling us shit like: to much is given, much is required? Well, you have to *give* people time to see your talent, then you can *require* a big ass check when they decide to buy your shit."

I laughed at her version of an inspirational pep talk, but I got what she was saying. "Thank you for that laugh. I really needed it," I told her.

"That's what I'm here for. Now that I got you out of your funk, you can repay my kindness by going out with me Saturday, and before you try to lie, remember that I know your work schedule, and you are always off on weekends. And since I'm the only person you really hang with, you can't say you have other plans."

"To where exactly?" I questioned, giving her the side eye. Her idea of going out was totally different from mine, and I didn't feel like ducking and dodging bullets.

"I would tell you, but I'd rather not. So be ready on Saturday around ten, and wear something sexy too. Now if you will excuse me, my man just told me he needs my sexy ass, so I'll holla at you later." She walked back into the living room, grabbing her purse and heading toward the door. "Don't forget what I said, and don't try to make up an excuse about not coming. I would hate to fight yo' ass, but I will. Love ya." She blew me an air kiss before she closed the door. I loved my cousin, but she had another thing coming if she thought I was about to spend one of my off days doing only God knows what with her.

****

I checked the time on my phone to see if it was time for me to get off. I sighed in relief when I saw that it was indeed five o'clock. I grabbed my things from my desk and hurried to clock out so I could take my ass to Walmart to do some grocery shopping for the month. After saying my goodbyes to everyone, I got in my car and hightailed it out of there. Normally, I would've driven in silence, but since I had a relatively good day at work, I decided to play some music. Going through my playlist, I chose a Drake song and bounced in my seat to the beat until I made it to my destination.

I pulled up my grocery list from my phone as I pushed the buggy down the aisle. Making sure that I had everything I would need, I tried stuffing my phone back into my purse but not before I bumped into someone, dropping my purse and spilling a few things out of it. "Sorry," I said, picking my things up off the floor.

"Watch where the fuck you are going next time, wrinkling up my shirt and shit," I heard a deep voice say.

I took a deep breath to calm myself down before getting up to address this rude ass person. I knew that today was going a little bit too well for me. Was it too much to ask for a day without drama? This was the exact reason why I preferred to stay in the comfort of my own home where I could avoid going through shit like this. I opened my mouth to tell him a piece of my mind, but when I laid eyes on him, I was stuck as I watched him as he tried rub out the imaginary wrinkle on his shirt with a scowl on his face. This man was one of the sexiest men that I'd seen. Since I had to look up at him, I could tell that he had to be well over six feet tall because I wasn't a short girl. He had golden-brown skin with sandy-colored dreads in his hair that he had in a low ponytail that looked like they came to the middle of his back. His facial structure was shaped to perfection with a sharp jawline. He didn't have much facial hair, only a barely visible mustache and a few strands of chin hair. From what I could tell, he looked as if he worked out a lot from the bulging muscles in his arms, and don't get me started on the way he smelled. I could tell from the scent that whatever cologne he was wearing was expensive.

"Aye, you don't hear me talking to you? Are you deaf or dumb?" I heard his voice cut through my thoughts.

Snapping out of my daze, I looked at him with a frown plastered on my face. Sexy or not, he had me all the way messed up if he thought I was about to allow him to talk to me like he didn't have sense. "First of all, you need to lower your voice and address me like you weren't raised by a pack of wolves. Now, I apologized for bumping into you, and the civil thing for you to do was accept it and keep it moving, but instead of you doing that, you decided to keep standing here, throwing a fucking fit like a damn child over a funky ass shirt. So instead of entertaining you, I'm going to be the mature person and walk away before things turned ugly," I said, proud that I'd taken the adult approach.

I watched as he chuckled to himself before looking at me with death in his hazel eyes. The way that he was looking had me spooked a little, but I refused to let him see that, so I hid my fear and gave him my best 'resting bitch' face.

"Fuck all that shit you are talking about. You are lucky that you didn't get shit on my clothes and that I'm pressed for time, or else this whole situation would've turned out differently with how you just spoke to me. Just watch where the fuck you are going next time before you bump into someone that won't be as nice as I am," he warned, walking off.

After that encounter, I was annoyed beyond reasoning and so ready to get out this store and go home. Leave it up to a sexy man with a stank ass attitude to fuck up my day. Once I paid for my stuff, I put my things in the car, praying that I didn't see that rude ass dude again. Getting into my car, I drove in silence, trying to calm my anger down, but there was only one thing that could do that for me—painting.

# Ron

*I* drove through my city in my candy-apple old-school Chevy, bumping UGK, bobbing my head. Today had been a stressful and long ass day for me, and it was only about to get worse. I was told that some of my money was low from one of my runners, and I was on my way to see about the shit. Three things I couldn't tolerate were disrespect, liars, and a person who stole from me, and he had violated all of them, so I was about to show his ass what time it was. Finally making it to the warehouse that was located on the outskirt of the city, I killed the engine before hopping out my whip. I noticed that my boy and right-hand man, Justin, was leaning against his royal-blue Phantom, puffing on a blunt, texting on his phone. Once he saw me approach, he put out his blunt and placed his phone in his pocket.

"What's good, my nigga?" he asked, dapping me up.

"Shit. Not much, just ready to get this shit over with. I'm tired as fuck," I replied as we walked into the building together.

I had called a meeting today, so everyone that worked for me was in attendance. I took a seat at the head of the table with Justin sitting right next to me. I sat quietly as I observed everyone's facial expression. While some looked cool, calm, and collected, others looked like they were scared to even breathe too loud, and I could understand why. I rarely called meetings, but when I did, nine times out of ten, someone wouldn't be leaving. I located the face of the nigga who was stealing from me and noticed that he couldn't stay still for shit. He played with his hands, and I could tell that he was shaking his legs underneath the table as well. Thanks to my father, I was a pro at reading people's emotions through their facial expressions and body language. Everything on this nigga's body read guilty.

Deciding to break my silence, I spoke. "I know y'all niggas wondering why I called this meeting on short notice, so I'mma get straight to the point. It was brought to my attention that some of my money was looking a little bit low from one of my trap houses for the last two months. Ant, can you explain to me why you have been short?" I questioned, giving him a chance to defend himself even though I was pretty sure he knew that he wasn't leaving out of here alive.

He stopped playing with his hands long enough to look at me. Clearing his throat, he spoke. "The block been slow lately. The crackheads really ain't buying shit like they used to, and they always trying to get stuff on credit until their checks come in."

I chuckled to myself, a habit that I had whenever I tried to control my anger. "I find it very funny that you would say that. I had Justin take time out of his day to drive by the block any chance he could get, and he told me that it was always booming. And Justin doesn't have a reason to lie to me. So are you calling him a liar? I would think about my response long and carefully if I were you."

He nervously looked between Justin and me, getting ready to say something, but before he could open his mouth, I pulled my gun out and shot him in the head, instantly killing him. I watched as his body slumped over his seat. "Bone, you are now in charge of the north trap house. Meeting adjourned, and somebody clean up this shit."

I got up from my seat, making my way out the door with Justin behind me.

"What you about to get into?" he asked once we were both outside.

"About to get into some pussy and then head home to chill for the rest of the night. What about you?" I looked through my phone and saw a message from one of my hoes telling me she was ready for me, attached with a naked picture.

"I got my girl waiting on me at home to get there so she can feed and fuck me. Yo' ass need to find a stable bitch that can do that for you."

"Nawl, I'm good on that relationship shit. I'll leave that to yo' ass. I have my own system going that is working just fine for me. Don't forget we have business to handle tomorrow, nigga, while you trying to be laid up," I called out, getting into my ride.

"Do I ever forget? While you talking about me, you should make sure none of them Looney Tune ass bitches you fuck with don't try to make a come up off you for the next eighteen years," he said through his window before pulling off fast as hell. I did the same thing as well.

I pulled up at one of my lil' freaks named Amber's house and knocked on the door. As soon as the door opened, I saw Amber standing in the door with no clothes on. She pulled me in and began to unzip my jeans, releasing my semi-hard anaconda then she started going to work. I closed the door so I could really enjoy the sloppy toppy

I was receiving. It was feeling good as fuck, but I didn't make a sound.

I had long ago trained myself not to make noise when I had sex. A lot of woman complained when I did that shit, but I didn't give a fuck. I had seen way too many niggas get played out by a bitch they were fucking, telling everybody that would listen how they had them niggas crying out like bitches in the bedroom, and I wasn't about to have anyone saying that shit about me. Feeling myself about to buss, I grabbed the back of her hair and face fucked her until all my kids went down her throat. I watched her slurp up every drop of my cum with a smile on her face. She got up from her knees and led me to the couch in the living room. Already knowing how I wanted to see her, she got on all fours, looking back at me.

"I'm waiting on you, daddy," she said in a seductive voice.

I got a condom from my pocket. Before I could get it on the head of my dick, I heard her say we didn't need that. So I asked her to repeat that shit because, clearly, I misheard her.

"I said you don't need one. I mean, we have been fucking with each other for the past eight months. I'm not fucking nobody else but you, so I feel like we are at the point in our relationship that we don't need to use rubbers."

I looked at her as if she'd just grown three heads. Clearly, this bitch was mistaking me for someone else. "Did you smoke something before I pulled up? You are talking crazy as fuck right now. What you mean by 'a point in our relationship?' Last time I checked, this was a fuck thing, and my ass is single as fuck, so you can miss me with that bullshit you're spitting."

I pulled up my jeans and zipped them back up so I could leave. She had fucked up my whole mood. She got up from the couch and tried to stop me from walking out. "If you walk out that door, you don't have to worry about ever hearing from me again, and you can consider this thing that we have over," she threatened.

I laughed in her face. "Ma, let me put you up on game or something. That threatening shit only works on a nigga if he actually cares about your ass. And I couldn't care less about you. If you feel like you should leave, then do what you got to do. You think I'mma be fucked up just because you won't be fucking with me no more? I have bitches on the sidelines that's waiting for me to bless them with the dick. Every time I dismiss one bitch, I bounce back with two. How you think I got you? Somebody got laid off," I schooled, moving her to the side so I could exit the door, leaving her standing there and cursing me to every name she could think of.

I made it to my house and went straight to the shower. I had to wash all of the day's stress off my body. After I was done, I warmed up a plate my mother dropped off for me before I left the crib this morning. Grabbing a beer out the refrigerator, I made my way upstairs to my bedroom. I turned my TV on and changed the channel from the sports channel to CNN to catch up on the latest news. I liked knowing what was going on in this crazy ass world that we lived in, especially with that dumb ass president that these stupid ass people elected. I was far from a dumb nigga. In school, my GPA was never less than a 4.0. I even skipped two grades. I had a Bachelor's and Master's degree in political science. I had the best of both worlds. I was street, but I always could engage with the elite, such as doctors, lawyers, politicians, and still hold my own.

Finishing up my food and gulping down the rest of my beer, I threw my trash away, turning off everything in my room, including the TV. I lay in the dark, thinking to myself. I needed a damn vacation, and I was planning on taking one real soon. All the stress from the street life was starting to wear me down. I was giving myself until the age of twenty-eight to retire from this shit, which was in three years.

I had enough money to get out now, but I wanted to make sure that I was set for life. I couldn't see myself doing this shit until I was old and gray like most niggas did. The smartest thing any nigga could do that was involved in the drug game was collect as much money as he could and get out while he still had the option to. My money was already making money due to the fact that I had my own legal business, and I invested in a lot of different stocks and small businesses.

When I retired, I planned on going around the world at least twice and then living in my mansion that I was currently building from the ground up on some land I purchased a few years back. I had thoughts of having a family of my own I could share it with, but I quickly dismissed that bullshit. Since I was the only child, my mother had plenty conversations with me about settling down and getting in a relationship so she could have some grandkids. I told her ass that she better get a puppy and pretend like it was a baby. She even went as far to hook me up with some girls that went to the church she attended.

Amber's nasty ass was one of them, and you could only imagine how the others went. I didn't think I'd ever be able to trust any bitch. I'd seen too many trifling, grimy ass female to ever give my heart to and bless them with my kids. That's why I said I was good on that relationship shit. It was a headache anyways. I didn't have the time or the patience to listen to a grown ass woman whine about irrelevant shit all day. I already had a fucked-up attitude, and that would just heighten it. Nawl, I wasn't built for that. I was happy getting my dick sucked, fucking, and leaving. If they wanted to act out, they got replaced. Point. Blank. Period. I yawned, closing my eyes and eventually falling asleep.

***

"Ooh, hell nawl! Nigga, we need to roll out now!" Justin shouted, looking at something on his phone.

"What the fuck you doing all that screaming for, and why do we need to roll out?" I asked, paying attention to the football game we were in the middle of playing before his ass started spazzing out.

"Tori ass thinks I'm playing with her. I told her hardheaded ass not to go out nowhere dressed like that. Look at this little ass shit she got on."

He tossed the phone over to me so I could see what he was talking about. His girl was on Snapchat, twerking on a table, with a little ass dress that barely covered her ass. You could tell that her ass was tipsy, because she almost fell trying to get off the table, but luckily, someone caught her. I threw the phone back in his direction, shrugging my shoulder. I didn't have those types of problems, so I didn't know what to tell him.

"Come on. Let's go," he said, already heading toward the door.

"Why can't yo' ass go by yourself?" I questioned. We had just got done handling business, and I just wanted to chill for the rest of the night, not get involved in this nigga's relationship problems.

"For one, I rode with yo' ass. Two, yo' stingy ass don't let nobody drive your cars. Three, we both know that you ain't about to let me pull up to the club by myself. So like I said before, nigga, let's go."

"Man, damn. Come on." I groaned, tossing the controller on the couch. I grabbed my keys off the coffee table and headed out. I was so fucking pissed. Here I was, going on a damn dummy mission with my boy at one in the morning. Justin better be lucky he was my nigga, or I would've told his love-sick ass to call an Uber and have them drop him off at the club by his damn self.

Once we made it to the club, I parked right in front of the entrance. We both made sure we were strapped just in case some shit popped off that was out of our control. We hopped out of my whip, walking straight to the door, bypassing everyone that was in line. I gave a head nod to the bouncer and he let us in.

The place was crowded as fuck. I didn't know how this nigga planned to find his girl through this thick ass crowd. One of Young Thug's song boomed through the speaker as females twerked their asses to the beat and niggas tried to run game. I just shook my head at this shit, finding it very comedic. I wasn't a club type of nigga. That shit didn't excite me like it did most niggas. I would rather travel; that's what my mind was on. The only times I ever went was when it was my birthday or one of my peoples were celebrating theirs. It was too much fake shit that happened in there, from niggas flexing like they had money to thirsty bitches looking for their next come up. I preferred to stay out of places that would have niggas thinking that they could run up on me or that would land me on the FEDS radar.

I looked toward Justin as he looked around, searching for his girl. I guessed he had finally spotted her, because he took off like a bat in hell, pushing people out of his way, and I was right behind him. When we finally made it to her, she was sipping on a pink looking drink, rapping to the song.

Justin walked up to her, yanking her out of her seat. "What I tell yo' ass about going out in public, showing all these lame ass niggas what's mine? Bring yo' ass on before I have to hurt you in this bitch."

"You ain't gon' do shit to me. I am a grown ass woman, and if I want to go out butt ass naked, I will. Ain't that right, Sasha?" she slurred, looking over to the girl that was sitting beside her. From the look on lil' mama's face, she looked like she wasn't enjoying herself at all. If I had to bet my money, I would say that her girl forced her to come out with her tonight.

"Don't put me in this," she said, crossing her arms with her face frowned up, mumbling something under her breath. Something about her seemed real familiar to me. Did I know her from somewhere? I never forgot a face.

Justin pulled his girl closer to him and whispered something that she only could hear. Whatever he said to her caused her to get her act together real quick, because she grabbed her purse and marched out the door with her friend with her.

Getting in my car, I pulled off. We rode in silence until Tori's drunk ass said she was hungry and wanted some Waffle House. Justin definitely owed me one for this shit. I kept stealing glances at ol' girl through the rearview, trying to place her face. I wasn't going to front; she was a cutie from what I could tell, but it was dark, so I had to see her in the light to reach my official verdict. Once we made it to Waffle House and got seated, I got a chance to fully take in her looks.

She had a medium brown-skinned complexion that looked smooth and soft as hell, dark-brown eyes that held innocence to them, and thick, kissable lips. Her dark-black hair was in a thick curly fro that covered half of her forehead like bangs with brown-colored ends. I had peeped her body while she was walking in front of me. She was on the petite side with barely any ass and breasts, but it looked good on her, and that was saying a lot coming from me because I was an ass man. Every hoe I fucked had a big ass, whether it was real or bought. I watched her looking out the window, not paying anyone at the table attention.

The waitress came up to the table to take our orders. "What can I get you guys?" she asked with a pen and paper in hand.

Tori was the first to order. "I'll get your All-Star meal with a lemonade to drink."

"I'll get the same," Justin said.

"I'll get your cheese steak with hash browns and Pepsi."

"Water will be fine for me," the girl named Sasha said before turning her attention back to the window. The waitress collected our menus then left to place our orders.

"You know you could've ordered anything off the menu, Sasha. I would've paid for it," Justin said to her.

She offered him a small smile. "I don't eat Waffle House food, but thanks for the offer."

While waiting on our food, Tori, Justin, and I engaged in conversation, cracking jokes and shit, while Miss Anti-Social remained quiet. I couldn't hold my comment so I finally spoke to her. "Are you always this quiet?" I asked her.

She looked at me and gave me the most hateful stare I thought I'd ever received from anyone. I didn't like that shit one bit. "Aye, do you have beef with me or some shit? You look familiar, but I know we didn't fuck around because you don't have enough ass for me. I must've turned you down, and now you are salty as fuck." I nodded my head. That had to be it.

"First of all, I wouldn't fuck you if your rude ass offered to pay me a million dollars. My vagina has standards, and your disrespectful ass doesn't meet the requirements. Since it's obvious you weren't raised by humans, I'mma break it down to you. Normally, when a person is not engaging in a conversation, it's usually due to the fact that they don't want to be fucking bothered. You could've took me rolling my eyes at you as a sign that I didn't want to talk to you and ignored me, but you just had to be childish and try to belittle me to help your bruised ego, but what should I expect from a man that throws tantrums over a damn shirt?"

Then it finally hit me. This was the same female that bumped into me the other day. I knew that she looked familiar, but I didn't really get a chance to get a good look at her before I walked off. What a small world. Even though I thought it was cute that she had the balls to try and check me yet again, she had me truly fucked up if she thought I was going to let that shit slide.

"Clearly, you must not know who the fuck I am, or you wouldn't be talking to me like you didn't value your fucking life. I went out of my way to try to make conversation with yo' nappy-headed ass, but you couldn't take that fucking stick you got up your ass out long enough to return the gesture, so I'll do you a favor. For the rest of the time we are around each other, I won't say shit to you and you do the same, but let me say this. If you come at me on some disrespectful type shit again, yo' peoples gon' be planning your funeral." I looked her in the eyes to make sure she understood that I was serious. I saw a glimpse of fear in her eyes before she rolled her eyes and told Tori to let her out of the booth.

"Did you really have to go there with her?" Tori questioned, following behind her girl.

"Damn, man, did you have to go that hard on that girl? She is cool people," said Justin, shaking his head.

I shrugged my shoulders, not giving a fuck about what he had to say. She talked to me like I wasn't shit, and like I said before, I didn't tolerate disrespect from any-fucking-body.

Our food had finally come out, and I didn't waste any time digging in. I hadn't eaten since this morning, and I was about to tear this food up. We finished our food, and I noticed that Tori and her friend hadn't come back, which was fine with me. The waitress came to give us the check. Justin told her to give him a to-go box so he could pack up his girl's food. I noticed shorty was giving me the googly eyes, but I paid no mind to it. That girl had given me a fucking headache with her fly ass mouth. We paid and left.

"You better tell your peoples to bring their asses on before they get left," I said once we were in the car.

"They been left. Tori texted me and said Sasha called an Uber, and she left with her about thirty minutes ago. On the real, you didn't have to go at her the way you did. She is really a cool ass girl from what I seen from her through the years I've been with Tori. You shouldn't have took offense to the way she was acting. She is always quiet around people that she don't know. She did me the same way, but she eventually got comfortable around me, but I guess since y'all met on fucked up terms, then she just didn't have shit to say around yo' ass," he tried to explain.

"Yeah, yeah. Whatever, nigga. Where you want me to drop you off at?" I asked, still not giving a fuck about what he had to say pertaining to that stuck-up hoe.

"Where else do I have to go? Take me to the crib."

I dropped him off and headed to my house to get a few hours of sleep before I had to wake my ass back up. I still felt some type of way about how that girl addressed me. I hoped this was our last encounter with each other, and if it wasn't, and she came at me like that again, I couldn't be held accountable for what I might do to her ass.

# $\mathcal{S}asha$

$\mathcal{I}$ walked through the mall, trying to pass time since my car was getting a much-needed oil change. I had an Uber drop me off because I wasn't about to be sitting in that place for almost two hours. I went into some of my favorite stores, looking through their seasons collection. It was starting to get cold outside, and I had yet to buy any new clothes for the winter. Even though I said that I wasn't going to buy anything, I ended up walking away with two large bags. I looked at my watch to see if I had time for one more store before I had to go back to get my car. Having only forty minutes to spare, I decided to make my last store be Bed, Bath, and Beyond. I was almost out of the candles that I used when I painted. Before I could walk in, I heard my name being called. I looked over my shoulder and saw that it was Kendrick jogging toward me. I tried quickening my pace, but he caught up to me, grabbing my arm.

I snatched my arm out of his grasp and threw him a hateful look. "Don't touch me again," I said through clenched teeth.

"I see you still on the bullshit. Look, I know I fucked up, but you should be over that shit by now. I mean, it happened damn near two months ago."

"Are you that stupid? You expect me to get back with you after you cheated on me? Do me a favor and go jump off a cliff and land on some pointy ass rocks," I said, trying to walking away, but he pulled me back, gripping my arm hard as hell.

I tried getting away from him, but he tightened his large hand around my arm. "I tried giving your ass space, but this shit here is getting real old. I miss you, and I want to get back to where we was before you got in your damn feelings and tried to break up with me."

"You can't be serious right now. We are over. Now let me go before I start screaming," I threatened. I didn't know what had gotten into him, but this wasn't the same person that I was with for three years. The person I was looking at now was someone I didn't even know.

"Did you not hear what I just said to yo' ass? Come on so we can work this shit out!" he shouted, scaring the shit out of me.

We had gotten into a tugging match with each other. I wasn't going anywhere with his ass. I thought someone would've intervened, seeing as how I was damn near screaming, but I had to remember where we were. He had gotten me almost to the exit, and that's when I heard someone finally stepping in to help me. Thank God, I thought to myself.

"Aye, my nigga, she said let her go."

I knew that voice. I looked up and saw that it was that sexy asshole that was friends with Justin. This was my first time seeing him since the Waffle House incident where he had threatened to kill me. He was looking extra sexy today. He was dressed casual in a blue hoody, dark denim jeans, with some blue and white Jordans on his feet, and his dreads hung freely over his shoulders. I never thought I would ever say this, but I was happy to see him.

"Who the fuck—oh, my bad. What's up, Ron?" Kendrick asked, changing his tone when he saw who it was, making me wonder who exactly this man was. "My girl and I just having a little argument. That's all. You know how these women get," he responded, trying to downplay the situation.

"Stop saying that. I'm not your girl anymore, so leave me alone," I corrected, still trying to remove my arm from his strong grip.

"I would hate to repeat myself, so I would advise you to do what the fuck I said," Ron replied in a calm but deadly tone.

I felt my arm being released. Kendrick looked as if he wanted to say something but decided against it. When he finally walked away, I released the breath I didn't even know I was holding. I turned to thank Ron, but he had already walked away. I ran to try to catch up to him, but it was no use. He was already gone.

Standing outside of the mall, I waited on my Uber to pull up so I could leave. I rubbed the bruise on my arm that Kendrick left where he had gripped it. I sighed. I couldn't blame anyone but myself for this. There were plenty of signs that showed me I needed to leave, yet I stayed. Ugh. I could truly say that I was stupid for that.

The wind started to blow, causing me to shiver. I hugged my body, trying to keep warm. I knew I should've worn a jacket today, but I just had to be hardheaded and wear a short-sleeved shirt. I looked at the Uber app on my phone, wondering where the driver could be. He was already ten minutes late. Getting ready to go back and wait on the inside, I saw a red Chevy, with a loud engine, bumping UGK, pull up in front of me. I knew that it wasn't the car of my Uber driver, because he had a Honda. I tried looking through the window to see who this person was, but the tint was so dark that I couldn't see anything. The driver rolled down the passenger window, and to my surprise, it was Ron. His mouth was moving, but I couldn't hear him over the loud music.

"What!" I yelled over the music.

He turned down the music. "You looking like yo' ass about to freeze with that lil' ass shirt you have on. Don't tell me you out here hoeing?"

Instead of saying something smart back, I chose to bite my tongue. I didn't have the energy to argue with him today, and if I was being honest with myself, he scared the shit out of me. From our two encounters before today, I could tell he had a few loose screws. Who was I kidding? His screws were missing.

"No, I'm waiting on my Uber to get here so I can go pick up my car, but I guess he is running late," I replied, looking around to see if I could spot the car.

"Hop in. I'll take you to wherever your car is at," he offered. I gave him a skeptical look. Surely this had to be a joke or something. "I can just leave yo' ass standing out here to freeze. I got shit to do, and you are holding a nigga up. Are you getting in or not?"

Weighing my options, I decided to get in the car with him. I didn't want to be out much longer than I already was. The warm air greeted my skin as soon as I entered the car. I gave him the directions to the place my car was as soon as we pulled off. He turned the music back up, and I silently started rapping the words of UGK's "Pocket Full of Stones." Thanks to my dad, I was practically raised off the late 80's, 90's, and early 2000's hip hop music. Whenever we were at home or driving around, that's the only thing he played. Even now, when I went home to visit, he played it.

"What you know about this shit?" he questioned as he turned down the volume. I guess he noticed me rapping along to the song.

"Boy, please. I'm not new to this; I'm true to it. I could rap this song in my sleep," I bragged. His mouth formed into a smile, and for the first time, I noticed that he had a nice set of teeth that were white and straight. Call me weird, but you could tell a lot about a person based on how well their teeth looked.

"Aight, whatever you say, ma," he said, laughing a little.

Even his laugh was sexy. I started feeling little butterflies flying around my stomach. *What the hell was wrong with me? I had to snap myself out of it.* This was the same asshole that basically threatened my life a while ago, and now I was over here feeling like a school girl with her first crush.

"You aren't going to kill me, are you?" I questioned nervously.

He looked over at me before turning his gaze back toward the road. "That's depends on you and that smart-ass mouth of yours." Judging by his answer and the stone expression he wore, I didn't need any more help to convince me that this man was serious.

I cleared my throat. "Well, thank you for helping me out back there. I know I'm not one of your favorite people, but you still helped me, so I wanted you to know that I really appreciate you for that, and thanks for the ride as well."

He ignored my comment and turned the music back up, signaling the end of our conversation. He pulled up to the car shop, and I grabbed my things and thanked him again for dropping me off. He gave me a simple head nod before driving off.

****

"He did what now?" Tori asked while braiding my hair. I was chilling at her house while she styled my hair in some black and brown box braids as I gave her the rundown of what happened at the mall the other day between Kendrick and me.

"He was trying to get me to go with him to God knows where, and he even left a bruise on my arm," I explained. "I don't know what's gotten into to him, but the way he was acting that day had me scared. Even when we had our arguments in the past, he never was that aggressive, and he damn sure didn't put his hands on me like that."

"Oh, hell nawl! He has some fucking nerves, placing his hands on you like that. The next time I see his ass, I'mma light him up like the Fourth of July. He got us all the way fucked up," she said, amping herself up. She had always been protective over me; I guess since she was two years older, she felt like it was her job to watch over me.

"Ouch!" I shouted as she pulled on the braid she was working on a little too rough.

"My bad, girl, but that shit just pissed me off. Ole fuck ass nigga. I'm still going to bust a cap in his ass, though, for fucking with you."

"Please don't," I said. I knew that she would really shoot him if given the chance to. "He's not even worth it, and I don't want to have to bail you out of jail and lie on the witness stand for you."

"You knew," she replied, causing both of us to laugh.

"I don't know what would've happened if Ron didn't come from out of nowhere and scared him off."

She stopped braiding my hair. "What do you mean, Ron came from out of nowhere?"

"Like I said, he scared Kendrick off and then walked away. Then when I was waiting on Uber outside the mall, he offered me a ride to the car shop and I took it."

She was now standing in front of me. "You mean psycho ass Ron? The same Ron that threatened to kill yo' ass a few months ago?" she questioned, looking shocked.

"Yes, that would be him. It was weird, though. The way he talked to me a couple months ago, I would've thought he disliked me just as much as I did him, but then he goes out of his way to help me. I don't know. It just seemed odd is all. What exactly do you know about him?" I asked curiously. I tried to make it sound casual even though I wanted to know everything there was about him.

Tori smiled, giving me a knowing look before walking around the chair to continue with my hair. "Well, for starters, I have never heard of him helping anybody out that's not a part of his crew. To be honest, no one really knows that much about him, not even the bitches that he fucks. He is hella private and low-key. He doesn't go out much, and he keeps his circle small. I'm talking about damn near a period, small. And I know that the worst thing you can do is get on that nigga's bad side. I've heard a few stories here and there of people that disrespect him in some form, and let's just say they came up missing."

"You never asked Justin about him since they are friends and whatnot?"

"Hell nawl. When I'm with my man, the only discussion we have is about us. We don't need to talk about other people; plus, I'm pretty sure if I were to bring up Ron in a conversation, he wouldn't tell me shit. Don't tell me you are feeling him."

"What? No. What would I look like, feeling someone that is damn near a psychopath? I just asked you a simple question." *Maybe I should've kept my thoughts to myself.*

"Mm hmm. Whatever you say, Sasha. I'm just going to say this, and it'll be the end of this conversation. Ron is different from the men you are used to dealing with. He's not about to be on no lovey-dovey type shit like the rest of these niggas. He will fuck you and move on to the next like it's nothing. I don't have to tell you how crazy he is, because you already experienced that for yourself. And if I'm being completely honest, I don't think you could handle him anyways. You try to act hard, but you are soft as hell. You don't need those types of problems that come along with him," she warned me. "But if somehow you do choose to go down that road, I will be there for you just like I was with Kendrick's lame ass."

I let everything she said marinate, and she was completely right. He might have helped me out, but he was still the same person that cursed me out for bumping into him by accident. I couldn't lie and say that the attraction wasn't there, but everything that looked good didn't mean that it was good for you. I didn't even know why I was overthinking this. He was probably messing with a bunch of women anyways. I was just going to stick to my original plan and focus on getting myself together. The last thing I should've been doing was entertaining the thoughts of another trifling man.

"Are you still coming with me to Georgia for Thanksgiving?" I asked, changing the subject.

"Of course, I am. You know I wouldn't miss Aunt Lisa's cooking for nothing in the world. That woman can throw down—too bad yo' ass didn't inherit that gene. I'm still trying to figure out how you lived with her for eighteen years and can't cook."

"Don't come for me. God gave everyone a special talent, and mine just so happens to be drawing. It's not like I can't eventually learn how to cook. Plus, that's what I got you for." I laughed.

"Girl, bye. I won't be cooking for yo' ass forever. You better start watching the cooking channel."

The door opened.

The alarm system sounded off, alerting us that someone came in. A few seconds later, Justin appeared around the corner, dressed in his usual attire, which consisted of a fitted cap, some denim jeans, a Gucci shirt, and a fresh pair of shoes. Justin was very attractive. He stood at six three with a rich-chocolate complexion that looked smooth and blemish free. He had somewhat bushy eyebrows, piercing black eyes, a long beard that women nowadays went crazy over, and a set of straight white teeth. He was very muscular as well but not in an over-the-top kind of way. To put it plain and simple, he was fine.

There had been plenty of occasions where Tori called my phone being angry that she had to check some female who tried to talk to Justin while they were out together. She voiced several times how she sometimes hated the attention that he always got from females, which I didn't understand, because she got the same amount of attention from other dudes. My cousin was beautiful. We had the same medium-brown skin tone, natural arched eyebrows, and full lips, but that's where it ended. She was taller than me by two inches at five nine, and where I was on the skinny side, she had ass and breasts for days. Her hair was in small dreads that stopped a little bit past her shoulders. She wanted them at a certain length, so whenever they would start to grow, she cut them.

"What's up? What y'all in here doing?" he asked, walking over to Tori, giving her a kiss.

"I'm just putting some braids in Sasha's hair. What are you doing here so early? I expected to see you later tonight. Now I got to tell my side nigga not to come over," she joked.

"Aye, don't get fucked up while you trying to be funny and shit. Let me find out yo' ass brought another nigga in the house I pay the bills in and see what happens. Matter of fact, let me go check the cameras to see if you were stupid enough to do some shit like that." We watched him as left the room, headed toward the stairs.

Making sure he was out of hearing range, I spoke. "Did you really plan on having another dude over here?"

She burst out laughing. "Nawl, I just wanted to make him angry so he could take it out on my pussy. Fuck that 'making love' shit tonight; I'm trying to not be able to walk straight for a couple of days." I shook my head at my crazy cousin. Only she would think of some mess like that.

"I really worry about you sometimes. I'm convinced that Aunt Keri stood in front of the microwave one too many times when she was pregnant with you."

"Yeah, yeah, yeah. Let me finish your hair so I can get my cat scratched." I couldn't do anything but shake my head at her.

\*\*\*

"Okay, class, that's all for today. You guys did a great job, and make sure you ask your parents to put your beautiful paintings on their refrigerators, okay?" I said to my students.

"Okay!" they yelled unison.

I dismissed the class and watched as they exited the room one by one. I started cleaning up the mess that my students had created from all the paint they used. I taught an art class at the recreational center once a month on Saturdays for eight- and nine-year-old children. I stumbled upon this job about eight months ago. I usually went here to exercise, and one day, I noticed that they had a sign up and were looking for someone that would take over the class for art, so I took it, and I was glad I did. It was one of the best decisions I'd made. It brought me joy to see how excited my kids were when they created something. Seeing that reminded me how I was around that age. I felt good inside, knowing that for two hours, they could get away from their problems, whether it be from home or school. After I was finished cleaning and packing everything, I turned off the lights and locked the door. I walked outside and noticed that one of my students was standing in front of the place by himself, holding his picture in his hands.

"Hey, Ryan. Why are you standing out here in the cold by yourself?" I asked.

"I'm waiting on my big cousin to come and get me since my mama had to work today," he said, rocking from left to right.

I couldn't leave him out here by himself, so I decided to wait for him until his cousin came. "Do you mind if I wait with you?"

He shook his head, saying no.

"Did you enjoy class today?" I asked, trying to spark up a conversation.

"Yeah," he replied, smiling. "I always like your class. You are my favorite teacher."

"Thank you, and you are one of my favorite students." I smiled, pinching his cute chubby checks.

He started giggling, showing off his snaggle teeth.

A few minutes later, a black Bentley stopped in front of us. The driver opened the door, and my breathing became shallow when I saw who it was. Ron climbed out the car and headed directly toward us. *Was it possible for a man to look sexier every time I saw him?* I questioned myself. When he got within distance of us, I instantly smelled his scent, causing my hormones to jump a little.

I watched him as he bent down to address Ryan. "Sorry for being late, lil' man. I forgot that I'd promised your mama that I would pick you up today, but I'll make it up to you," Ron said. I had to do a double take to make sure that I wasn't tripping. The man before me sounded so gentle and compassionate, not like the cold-hearted asshole I'd known him to be. I guess kids did bring out the gentler side of people.

Ryan smiled at him. "It's okay. Ms. Sasha waited out here with me. Look at the picture I painted today," he said, showing off his picture to Ron.

Ron looked up at me like he finally noticed that I was standing there. Trying to avoid his gaze, I focused my attention on the passing cars.

Slowly rising from the kneeling position that he was in, he stood up, towering over me. "Ryan, go get in the car before you get sick. I'll take you to get some candy before you go home. Aight?" I heard him tell Ryan.

"Yay! Bye, Ms. Sasha. I'll see you at the next class." He gave me a hug then ran to get in the back seat of Ron's Bentley.

I started walking off but felt a hand wrap around my wrist. "I appreciate you waiting with him until I came."

"It was nothing. It wasn't like we were waiting out here for that long anyways." I nervously smiled, prying his grip from around my wrist so he couldn't feel me shaking.

He stared at me intensely without uttering a word, making me wonder what thoughts were going through his head. I started to feel uncomfortable. "Well, if that's all, I'm going to head out."

He pulled his phone out of his pocket and handed it to me. "Put your number in," he commanded.

"Wait. What?" I asked, unsure if I was hearing him correctly.

A frown formed on his handsome face. "Damn, there yo' ass go, acting deaf again. I said put your number in and hurry up. It's cold as fuck out here, and I don't have time to be waiting on your slow ass."

He had to be crazy if he thought I was going to give him my number now after the way he just spoke to me. The small crush I did have on him quickly went away. I handed him back his phone. "Nawl, you good," I replied.

He chuckled to himself. "Aight, bet," he said, walking over to his car. He pulled off moments later.

For all the years I'd been living here, I never ran into him, not once, but all of a sudden, I was seeing him everywhere I went. I didn't know what the universe was trying to do, but I did know one thing. The next time I saw him, I was going to run in the opposite direction.

I stepped inside my apartment and instantly fell on the couch. Today had been a bad day for me. First, I was twenty minutes late for work, causing me to get five points, all due to the fact that I had forgotten to put my phone on the charger, and my battery ended up dying. Then I had to deal with every last person that I had assisted cursing me out to everything that they could think of like it was my fault they didn't pay their bills on time. When I went on break, I called myself trying to make a strawberry smoothie, but instead of going in my mouth like it was supposed to, it landed on my white shirt that I'd just purchased. I needed a break from life.

Getting up from my couch, I headed to my room to get out of my work clothes and change into my painting clothes, which consisted of a pair of black tights and an oversized black T-shirt that looked as if it would swallow my body. I made my way into the other room in my apartment, which I nicknamed Sasha's World. I already had my tools and board set up, so the only thing that was left for me to do was light my vanilla-scented candles. Putting in my headphones, I went to my Apple music playlist and clicked on the singer H.E.R.'s album. Listening to the smooth sounds of her tone and melody, I began to paint. I felt this unexplained energy run through my body as I mixed and matched lines, shapes, and colors until they formed into what I perceived as perfection.

I was so into painting that I didn't even notice that Tori was standing behind me until she touched my shoulder, and I nearly jumped out of my skin. I took my headphones out of my ears. "That shit is not funny. You almost gave me a heart attack," I said, watching her crack up.

"That's what your ass get for having me knocking at the door for almost ten minutes. You better be lucky that I remembered where you kept your extra key at, or you would've been paying for another window."

"Correction. *You* would've been paying for another window, not me," I corrected.

She rolled her eyes. "Yeah, whatever. Anyways, I came over here to see if you wanted to go out and eat with me. I would've went by myself, but I wanted some company."

"Don't you have a man that you can go with?" I honestly didn't feel like going anywhere. I just wanted to relax.

"Yeah, I do, but since I live with the nigga, it's natural for us to get tired of each other. And I wanted to chill with my favorite cousin." She smiled at me.

"How about we stay in? I have some stuff here that you can cook."

Her face frowned up with disgust. "Don't nobody want that nasty ass health shit that you buy. I want a fat ass burger, some big salty ass fries on the side, with a large sugary ass glass of sweet tea."

I cringed at her description of the food she wanted to consume. The thought alone had my teeth hurting. "I'm not going to say anything when you gain five hundred pounds from eating all that; just know that I am not going to be rolling you around everywhere, but I'll go," I said, giving in. Knowing my cousin, if I didn't agree to go, she would probably get on my nerves until I put her ass out. The way I looked at it was, the faster we left, the faster I could come back to finish my painting and watch a little TV before I went to bed. I changed into some regular black ripped jeans, black Converse, and a black hoody. I didn't want my box braids in my face, so I opted to style my hair in a high bun. I checked my appearance. Satisfied with how I looked, we headed out the door.

After debating on what restaurant we should go to, we eventually chose Buffalo Wild Wings. I wasn't that hungry, so I ordered some wings to go while Tori pigged out on her wing platter. The girl could clear a whole plate in less than five minutes. I honestly thought that all Tori's food went to her ass, because she didn't have any stomach.

"Slow down. That food ain't going nowhere," I joked.

"Kiss my—" She stopped mid-sentence, focusing her attention on something behind me. I turned to see what she was staring at so hard. "What are you looking at?" I asked, confused.

Instead of answering my question, she left her seat in a hurry with an angry look on her face. I got up and followed closely behind her. We stood behind a couple of dudes that looked to be entertaining a couple of females in the bar area. I stood beside my cousin, wondering what about this was making her upset.

"So this is what yo' dusty ass do when you claim that you are busy, huh? Entertain these busted-down ass females?" Tori yelled, causing the laughter to stop and the men to turn around in their seats, revealing their faces. Now I understood why she rushed over here. It was Justin, Ron, and another man that I'd never seen before. The girl that was sitting next to Justin had her hand on the upper part of his arm while she smiled in his face. When she saw us, her smile dropped immediately.

"What the fuck you are talking about? Do you see me smiling in another bitch face? No. So kill that shit," he said standing in front of her.

She kissed her teeth and rolled her neck. "Nigga, do I look like boo-boo the fool to you? Is it a sign on my forehead that says dumb bitch? If it's not what I think it is, then why was the bitch hand on your arm? Matter of fact, why are you allowing these bitches to touch yo' ass, period?"

"Like I told you, I'm not entertaining no bitch but yo' loud mouth ass," he said through gritted teeth. "You are causing a fucking scene. Go the fuck home and we'll discuss it there."

"You got me all the way fucked up if you think I'm about to leave without you. Nawl, nigga, we are a team, so when you leave, that's when I'm leaving." She looked toward the girl that was seated next to Justin. "Excuse me, but you see this nigga right here? This has been my dick for seven years, and I'm crazy over it. So if you don't want to see how crazy I will get over it, then I would advise you and your little friends to exit stage left."

The girl and her friends looked as if they were about to say something until Tori showed them her taser. "Like I said, you don't want these problems," Tori said. They got up from their seats, rolled their eyes at us, then left.

"Do you feel better now?" Justin asked sarcastically, returning to his original seat.

"Much better. Sasha, sit down. Now that those thirsty ass females are gone, it's more than enough room." And just like that, her mood had changed from angry to calm. I swear, I couldn't deal with her sometimes.

"No, you can stay here. I'll just go back to our table, and you can just come and get me when you are ready to leave," I said, not waiting for a response.

I was serious about avoiding Ron like he was a plague. I didn't want to be anywhere near him, because I was sure that if he came at me wrong, I would snap on him, and I was sure he would make good on his promise. I didn't want a person like that to be in my space, but I couldn't help the tingling I felt when I noticed the look that he was giving me while Justin and Tori went back and forth with each other.

I didn't want to seem like I was lonely, so I pulled out my phone and decided to read a few art blogs since I was now by myself. I was on my third blog before I felt the presence of someone standing in front of me. I didn't have to look at the person's face to know who it was; the expensive smelling cologne gave him away.

"So you gon' sit there and continue to pretend like I'm not standing here?" Ron asked with a smirk on his face. *Why did he have to be so damn fine?* I thought to myself. But I quickly remembered that I needed to stay away from him, so instead of entertaining him, I continued reading the blog. Next thing I knew, my phone was being snatched from my hands.

Sighing in frustration, I finally looked at him. "Are you always this childish?" I asked. "I thought we had a mutual understanding of 'I stay out of your way; you stay out of mine.' So could you please give me back my phone and make your way back to where you came from?"

Instead of doing like I asked, Ron sat in the seat in front of me. I should've known that it would be too nice of him to do as I asked. "And I thought *you* understood that I can do what the fuck I want to do, but apparently, yo' slow ass couldn't comprehend."

I rolled my eyes. "Well, since I have a strong feeling that you aren't going to leave anytime soon, and judging based off our encounters and your huge ego, if I try to get up and leave, you would forcefully stop me, we might as well make this interaction a pleasant one. So my first question is, why are you an egotistical asshole? Like, would it kill you to actually act like a decent person?" I asked, leaning back in my chair with my arms folded, awaiting his answer.

He stroked his chin between his thumb and index finger. "So that's how you really want to start off the conversation? I thought you wanted this interaction to be a pleasant one? That's like me asking yo' simple ass why you act like you have a stick up your lil' booty ass."

I could already see where this was headed, so I took another approach so I could possibly find out some type of information about him. "Are you an only child?"

He raised an eyebrow. "What make you ask me that?"

I shrugged my shoulders. "I don't know. I mean, you just have the attitude of one. The spoiled, arrogant, entitled attitude, like you was loved way too much as a child." He burst out laughing, and I gave him a confused look. "What are you laughing for?"

"That's the first time I've heard somebody say some crazy ass shit like that. How can a person be loved too much?" he inquired.

"I can't think of a way to explain it right now, but it's possible." I started laughing as well. "You still have to tell me if I'm right about my assumption, and I just want to go on record by saying, I made your mean ass not only smile but laugh."

"You better remember this moment because this shit won't happen again."

I stared at him, waiting for my question to be answered.

"What, man? Damn."

"Stop being so damn secretive and answer my question," I scolded.

"I'm the only child," he responded like he was annoyed to even answer it.

"See. Was that so hard?" I asked like a mother would do a child that didn't want to eat vegetable.

"Don't push your luck, girl."

I held my hands up in surrender while trying to hold in my giggles. Surprisingly, for the rest of our conversation, we didn't argue.

I was hoping that I would find out some more information about him, but he kept shutting it down, only answering the basic questions I asked him. By the time we were about to leave, he somehow managed to call his number with my phone, getting my number involuntarily. It was safe to say that my plan to stay away from him was a total failure, but a part of me was happy that it was.

# Ron

"That's game, nigga! Now run me my money," Justin said, slapping the pool stick down on the table after shooting the solid pool ball in the hole.

Bryan reached into his pocket and handed Justin the five hundred dollars they had betted on. "This some bullshit. How did you even make that damn shot?" Bryan groaned, obviously pissed off that he was out of some money even though five hundred dollars was like a penny to us.

"Because yo' boy got skills. I told you, you didn't want to see me when it came to pool, but it's always motherfuckers like you who I have to prove a point to."

I looked back at them, shaking my head. I didn't understand why those two even bet on anything at this point. It always ended the same damn way. One of them won, the other got mad, they almost come to blows, and I break it up. We were all chilling at Justin's house after making sure everything was good with the shipments and products. This was one of the routines we had developed over the years of knowing each other. On the rare occasion when it wasn't that much work to be done with the business, we would either chill at Justin's, Bryan's, or my house. These were the only two niggas that I fucked with on a friendship level. We'd known each other since the age of ten. We were damn near brothers. Our families were close since our fathers built a drug empire together, and naturally, they passed it down to us. I felt my phone vibrating in my pocket, alerting me that I had gotten a text. I saw the name and smirked. I opened the message.

**Sasha:** *I'm not sure if you are busy, but if you aren't, could you please save me from my boredom?*

**Me:** *What the fuck yo ass bored for? I thought you suppose to be at work?*

**Sasha:** *I am but its been a slow day. Literally there's nothing to do. Could you do me a favor?*

**Me:** *HELL NAWL. Who the fuck I look like?*

**Sasha:** *Come on, mean ass. Please. It's not that big of a deal.*

**Me:** *what you want?*

**Sasha:** *Make me laugh.*

I couldn't help but smile. This girl was truly a character. How was she just going to text and ask me if I could make her laugh? Most females that texted my phone wanted one thing, but making them laugh wasn't one. I sent her back the middle-finger emoji and laid my phone on the table. I resumed the football game that I was playing. We had become cordial with one another after having that conversation at Buffalo Wild Wings.

I was still trying to figure out what it was about her that had me doing stuff out of my character. That day at the mall when I saw her and ole boy get into it, I was about to walk away. Normally, I didn't get into other people's business, because I hated when people even inquired about mine, but when I saw the distressed look on her face, I couldn't just let it go. Then seeing her talking to my baby cousin outside, smiling, I felt something. I didn't know exactly what it was, but I wanted to know more about her; that's why I asked for her number, something I'd never done before. But she turned me down.

I wasn't going to lie and say that my ego didn't take a hit. I wasn't used to being denied over anything, so I was like fuck her. That night when Tori came over to our table, causing a scene and shit, I saw Sasha behind her, and I got that feeling again. I was glad that she went to the table by herself. It gave me a chance to pick her mind and see what it was about her that had me curious. I found out that she was a cool person—corny as hell sometimes—but she was cool. After I unlocked her phone, getting her number, I waited about a week or two before I hit her up, and we'd been talking since then.

It wasn't on any relationship type shit either. I still felt the same about that, but it was cool to talk to a woman that didn't talk about sex, celebrity drama, or makeup. We didn't talk about shit for real, but it was enough to let me know that she had her head on straight and wasn't one of these lazy ass bitches that just wanted to lay on their backs and fuck any nigga that was getting a little money.

"What you over there smiling about?" I heard Bryan ask me. Instead of answering, I continued to play the game.

"Sasha probably texted his ass or some shit. I heard that they have been getting real close over the last few months," said Justin.

"I know you lying." Bryan sounded surprised. "She must got

some bomb ass pussy for Ron to be fucking with her like that."

I was starting to get annoyed. "Damn, why y'all over there sounding like a bunch of gossiping ass females? Who I'm talking to ain't up for discussion. Worry about who y'all fucking, and get off of my dick."

It got quiet, and they burst out laughing. These niggas didn't take anything seriously.

"Damn, nigga. It's like that now? So it must be true. I never thought I'd see the day that a female would have you being secretive and shit," Bryan started it off.

"Ooohhh shit." Justin balled up his fist and placed it to his lips. "Don't tell me yo' ass caught feelings?"

"Nigga, are you smoking crack or some shit? Act like you know me. What I look like catching feelings for a chick I barely know? Don't get me wrong; she is a cool ass female, but that's it. I don't have the time or patience to babysit nobody feelings," I said, trying to dead the conversation. These niggas were really tripping on if they thought I had caught feelings. We only ever talked on the phone because both of us were always busy. I felt something for her, but I was pretty sure once I fucked, that feeling would go away.

"So since you don't care about her, you wouldn't mind if I get her number, see what she's talking about, right?" Bryan had a smirk on his face. I knew what he was trying to do, so I played right along with his ass.

I looked at him with a straight face. "I don't see why you asking me. Like I told you before, I'm not feeling her like that. Do you, my nigga."

Bryan and Justin gave each other a knowing look before collecting the pool balls to play another game. I ended the football game I was playing and chucked up the deuces. I had somewhere I needed to be.

Leaving from Justin's house, I texted Bria, a bad ass big-booty bitch that I fucked from time to time, letting her know that I was on my way and to be naked and waiting for me. I hadn't had my dick wet in almost two weeks, and I needed a release. I didn't consider myself a sex addict or a nymphomaniac, but I loved sex. What man didn't, though? Show me a man that said he was fine with going a week without fucking, and I bet you he is lying.

I pulled into her apartment building, and just when I was about to turn left, I saw Sasha getting some stuff out of her car. She looked like she was struggling a little. I parked my car in the nearest available parking area I could find and made my way toward her. Just as she was about to drop a bag she was carrying, I ran and caught it.

She looked startled before she realized that it was me. "What are you doing here? How did you know where I lived?" she asked curiously.

It took me a minute to answer because I was focused on how good she was looking. "I didn't. I was headed to fuck something, then I noticed you over here struggling and shit, so I decided to stop and help yo' lil' ass," I replied honestly. One thing people could say about me was that I was honest. I didn't see the point of lying to no-motherfucking-body. It wasn't like they could beat my ass anyways.

"Oh, well, I don't want to hold you up or anything, so you can just go. Thanks for getting my bag before it fell," she said. If I hadn't been paying attention, I wouldn't have caught the disappointed look on her face before she hid it.

She unlocked the door to her apartment, letting us in. She set her things down on the floor, and I couldn't help but to look at her little booty ass in those tights she was wearing. Even though she didn't have much ass, she had a cuff—something that could be gripped on to. I wondered if I hit her from the back, would it juggle? I was so caught up in my nasty ass thoughts of what I wanted to do to her that I didn't notice that she was standing in front of me with her hand on her hips, snapping her fingers to get my attention.

"Aye, don't be snapping at me like I'm a damn dog or something."

She rolled her eyes. "Well, I was calling your name, but it seemed like you couldn't hear me, so I had to do something to get your attention. You can go now. I don't want to hold you up from getting some."

She walked away from me, heading to her bedroom. I looked at my phone and saw that Bria had called and texted me twice. I already knew that she wanted to know where I was, so I didn't even bother opening her message. Deciding that I was going to chill here for a while, I took a seat on her couch, looking around her living room. She had paintings all over her walls. I wondered what the purpose of all these pictures was.

Some of the paintings were dope as hell. I figured she must be into shit like that to have them everywhere. A few minutes later, she came out from the back with some short pink shorts that showed off her long, slim, toned legs and a big oversized black V-neck shirt. Her braids were no longer hanging down; she had put them in a bun on top of her head. I watched her go into her kitchen and appear with a bottle of some green looking shit.

My face frowned in disgust as I watched her drink it. "What is that green shit you are drinking? It looks like some green shit that came out of somebody ass."

She swallowed whatever that was before she started laughing. "It's a smoothie I made. It helps me when I need an energy boost, and it's good for the body. It naturally cleans out the toxic things you put into your body as well."

"You wasted your breath saying all that unnecessary shit when you could've just said that you are backed up and haven't shitted in a while. Just let me know when you start to feel your stomach bubbling so I can bounce." I was serious. I knew I was immature for thinking this, but in my mind, I refused to believe that females had the same stinky ass shit we had coming out of our bodies.

Sasha sat down on the other couch that was beside the one I was sitting on and grabbed the remote from off the coffee table. "Shouldn't you be gone anyways?" she asked, scrolling through her channels, finally settling on an episode of *Martin*. I half expected her to turn to one of those fake ass reality shows females loved to watch now.

"I'll leave when I feel like it," I said, scooting my body down on the couch, making myself more comfortable.

She sighed before rolling her eyes and focusing on the TV, and I did the same. We laughed through the entire episode. *Martin* was one of those timeless shows that never got old. Once the show was over, she heated some pizza up in the oven and cut both of us a slice.

"Let me ask you something," I started off. "Why are there so many painting on your walls? Do you collect them or something?" I asked curiously.

She held up one finger, signaling for me to hold on while she chewed her food. Once she had swallowed and took a sip out of her water, she replied, "Yes, and no. I am a painter, and I painted every picture on my wall."

"You painted all of these?" I asked once again. She nodded her head. "I didn't know that you painted this kind of stuff. Some of these pictures are cool as hell." I was low-key kind of shocked. She didn't come across as the painting type. I mean, I didn't know how a painter should look, but the image I had in my head wasn't how she looked.

"Thank you. I don't know why, but that means a lot coming from you," she said, smiling at me. I felt my heart skip a beat. If I was an average nigga, and she smiled at me like that, I would have given her anything that she wanted.

"Why are you looking at me like that? Do I have something stuck in my teeth?" She covered her mouth.

"Nawl, I was just noticing how cute you were," I flirted.

She smiled before playing with her thumbs. I could tell just from her body language that she didn't know how to respond to what I just told her. Also, just from her reaction, I could tell that she was feeling me. I wasn't even surprised; I knew I looked good. We watched two more episodes of *Martin* before I saw her yawning. I looked at the time on my phone and saw that it was almost two in the morning. I didn't expect to be over here that long, but I wasn't tripping over it. I enjoyed chilling with Sasha. Being with her had me feeling all calm and shit.

"Wake yo' ass up, with your disrespectful ass. It's rude to fall asleep while you have company." I hit her thigh, causing a loud smack sound.

"Ouch! That hurts!" she yelled, rubbing her thigh.

I laughed at her trying to throw a tantrum. "You can't have a smart-ass mouth and cry like a baby over that soft ass hit that I just gave you," I said, feeling my phone vibrate. Bria texted me again, asking me if anything was wrong and if I was still coming. Instead of responding, I set it down beside me.

She glared at me then stuck up her middle finger. "I think it's time for you to leave. Plus, I'm pretty sure that your booty call is wondering where you are." She got up and headed to the door and opened it.

I walked up to her and closed the door before backing her into it. I placed both of my hands flat on the door above her head to make sure she couldn't escape. I moved my head toward her face, only stopping inches away from it. We were so close that I could hear her heartbeat through her chest. "I'm not going anywhere. I'm tired and I'm sleepy, so point me to your bedroom so I can lay my ass down," I said, fighting the urge to kiss those juicy lips of hers.

"I... I... I don't know w-hat you think this is, but if y-you think th-that I'm going to sleep with you, then you might as w-well go with your original plan and ride to that other girl's place," she stuttered.

I laughed at her trying to boss up.

"What are you doing all that stuttering for, huh? Your body and your words aren't matching. You want to know what I think? I think you want me to spend the night with you and fuck you until you fall asleep then wake you back up just to do it again," I said, whispering in her ear. Saying fuck it, I kissed her lips. I wasn't the kissing type at all, but her lips were calling my name.

I couldn't explain the tingling feeling that ran down my back as soon as our lips connected. Her lips were so fucking soft that I had to stop myself from biting them. Wanting more, I let my tongue enter her mouth, and she sucked on it with so much passion. I removed my hands from the door and grabbed her ass, pushing her body close to mine so she could feel the effect the kiss was having on me. I felt her slowly grinding against me, causing me to brick up even more.

I pulled away, creating some distance between us. If I didn't, I was pretty sure we would've been fucking. I ran my thumb across my lips while I watched her try to control her breathing. "Damn, girl, I got you out of breath like that from a kiss? Imagine how you will feel when I bless you with the dick." I smirked.

Without responding, she headed to her bedroom. I locked the door and turned off the lights before going in the same direction. I looked around her bedroom, nodding my head in approval. I half expected her room to be junky and have clothes thrown everywhere, but it was clean and smelled like vanilla or some shit. She had a king-size bed with a brown comforter that matched the curtains that hung on the windows. Her dresser was brown also, and the TV sat on top. I stripped down to my boxers I had on and made myself comfortable in her bed. She came out the bathroom and frowned up her face.

"What do you thinking you're doing? I thought I told you to

leave."

"Why did you go into the bathroom? I didn't hear the toilet flush, so I know that you didn't use it, not unless you are one of those nasty ass females that leave piss in your toilet, and I know your water was on because I heard the water in the sink running. That leads me to believe that I got yo' ass so wet that you messed up your panties." I watched her face as she changed from being angry to embarrassed. "You don't have to be ashamed. I have that effect on every woman I meet," I said cockily.

Sasha mumbled something under her breath before climbing in bed with me. She made sure she put some distance between us. Her ass was so close to the edge that I was sure if she rolled over, she would be on the floor. She reached on the nightstand and turned off the lamp that sat on it. We stayed this way for a while. I could hear her snoring softly on the other end of the bed. I didn't know what came over me, but I wanted to have her in my arms, so I scooted toward the middle and placed my arms around her body, careful not to wake her up. I exhaled loudly.

This was a first for me in many ways. I never slept at another person's house, let alone a woman's, other than my or my parents' home. And I damn sure didn't do this cuddling shit. Damn, what was this girl doing to me that had me feeling and acting like a bitch? I kept telling myself that she was a challenge and that I wanted to fuck her, but I knew deep down, it was something more, and I didn't think I was ready for what came with that. In my mind, I had only two choices—to explore what it was about her that had me feeling this way or fuck and be done with her. I wasn't about to make that decision tonight, so I let out a yawn and wrapped my arms around her and closed my eyes.

I woke up to the smell of food being cooked. I rubbed my eyes, looking around to see where I was at. It only took me a few seconds to realize that I was still at Sasha's place. Getting up from my comfortable place in her bed, I headed toward the bathroom to take my morning piss. Once I was done, I put on my clothes from the previous day and walked into the kitchen where I heard her on the phone talking to someone. Normally, I wouldn't eavesdrop on someone's conversation, but I was curious to know whom she was talking to and what were they talking about.

"I understand, sir, but all I'm asking is that you take a look at my portfolio. You'll see that I could be a great addition to your company," she said, stirring the eggs in the pan.

Suddenly, she stopped what she was doing. "Okay, I understand. Thank you for taking the time out of your day to answer my call." I watched her as she leaned against the wall with her eyes closed, looking defeated.

Deciding to make my presence known, I strolled in the kitchen and stood in front of her, taking in all of her beauty. Even through the sadness that was evident on her face, she was still cute as hell to me. I admired her for a few more seconds before she opened her eyes, gazing into mine. I noticed that her eyes were glistening with tears. She wiped her eyes and went back to the stove to finish cooking, completely ignoring me.

"What was that about?" I heard myself asking her.

She cleared her throat. "Umm... it was nothing that I'm not already use to. Are you hungry?" Sasha asked. I could tell she didn't want to talk about it, so I wasn't going to pressure her. If she wanted me to know, she'd tell me.

"Hell yeah," I responded.

"Well, sit down, and I'll fix you a plate."

I took a seat and pulled out my phone while I waited for her to finish. I had messages from Justin, Bryan, five of my hoes, and one from my mother. I opened her message to see what she wanted. My mother rarely texted me, and when she did, it was usually important.

*Mother: Whenever you get time, I need you to stop by the house today. I need to have a conversation with you.*

I'd head over there once I left here. I knew I hadn't done shit over the last couple months, so I knew that whatever she wanted didn't have shit to do with me. *Maybe my father fucked up again.*

Sasha set the plate of food in front of me. I looked down and saw what she had cooked. When I laid eyes on the eggs, sausage, pancakes, and hash browns, my mouth watered. I hoped it tasted as good as it smelled, or I was going to throw this whole plate in the trash. After I said my grace, I dug in. It wasn't the best that I had, but she had a little bit of skills.

I was almost done with my plate when I realized she wasn't eating anything. She had her hand underneath her chin, staring off into space like she was in a daze.

"Why you ain't eating anything?"

She shrugged her shoulders, continuing to stare at the wall.

Wiping my mouth with a paper towel, I turned her body toward me so we could be facing each other. "You've been quiet ever since you got off your phone, and it's starting to fuck up my mood. So tell me what's wrong before I leave yo' ass in here crying by yourself," I said in the nicest way I knew how.

She glared at me. "Do you always have to be an asshole about everything? Would it kill you to be a little bit nice for once in your life? If I'm fucking up your mood, then you can leave. I didn't even invite you here in the first place. You invited yourself. The door is that way, so feel free to leave," she spat, getting up from the table and going in the back, leaving me by myself.

I ran my hands down my face and counted to ten, trying to calm myself down from going back there and choking the shit out of her for talking to me like that. See, this was why I didn't bother with spending time with a female. They were too fucking emotional. Here I was, trying to see what was wrong with her stupid ass, and she spazzed out on me. Granted, I could've asked in a less hostile way, but at least I cared enough to ask. I had a half of mind to leave and be done with her sensitive ass, but something inside was telling me to go check up on shorty. I walked back to her bedroom and saw that she wasn't in there. I heard music coming from the other room across the hall, and I made my way in that direction.

When I opened the door, I was surprised to see her holding a paint board in one hand and a brush in the other. She was drawing what looked like to be a bunch of lines going in different directions.

My eyes roamed the room, admiring all the paintings that decorated the walls and half of her floor. I didn't know much about art, but anyone could see that this girl was talented. She painted with so much passion that I developed a newfound respect for her. Instead of interrupting her as she did her thing, I leaned against the door, waiting until she was done.

Finally, she put the paintbrush on her paint board thingy and laid them on a dresser. When she turned around, I started clapping my hands.

"What are you doing here? I thought I told you to leave. And what's with the clapping?"

I walked over to the board to get a closer look at what she had just painted. "Because I think you have talent when it comes to this shit. Have you ever thought about selling some of these painting to make a profit off of them? You could really make a career move out of this," I said.

She chuckled to herself. "It's funny that you mentioned that. That's what my life goal is to do, but it's not my time I guess. I sold a few, thanks to Tori posting them on her social media pages, but that's about it. I have to get ready for work, so I'll talk to you whenever." She left out the room. It was something about the way she said that last sentence that had me feeling like there was an underlying meaning to what she was saying.

I nodded my head before grabbing my keys and walking out the door. It was obvious that she wanted to be alone, and I was going to respect her wishes.

I went straight to my parents' house to see what my mother

wanted. Once I made it to the gate of their mansion, I typed in the code, allowing me to enter. I parked my car alongside my father's black Rolls Royce and hopped out. Walking into the house, I headed to the one room I was sure my mother would be in—her woman cave. Just like my father wanted his own space whenever my mother started to get on his nerves, my mother felt the same way.

I knocked before I opened her door and let myself in. My mother was sitting on her white couch, watching a home decorating show. When she saw me, she smiled and turned down the volume on the TV. My mother was in her mid-forties but didn't look a day over thirty. Her golden-brown skin was flawless and wrinkle free. She rocked her hair in a short finger-waved style, and her hazel eyes had a natural glow to them, and she had a smile that could melt ice.

"What up? You wanted to see me?" I asked, getting straight to the point.

"When you come into a room, the first thing you should do is say hey to the person and ask them how they are doing. I know I raised you better than that," she scolded.

"My bad. Hey, Mama. How are you doing? You eating good? Living right?" I joked, plopping down beside her.

She giggled, shaking her head. "Yes, I'm fine. Thanks for asking. Now, I know you are wondering why I asked you to come over here. I got a call from Amber yesterday, crying, telling me how much she loves and want to be with you, but you broke up with her and cussed her out because she said she wanted to have your child. Is there any truth to this?"

I had to laugh because, surely, this was a joke. "Is this seriously what you called me over here to talk about?" When I saw that she was wearing a straight face, I frowned up, feeling my anger rise.

"Yes, that's exactly what I called you over here for. Amber is a nice young lady, and I think that y'all would be perfect for each other. She comes from a good home, and she's not like these other fast-tailed girls you deal with. Just give her a chance," she pleaded.

I didn't want to disrespect my mother, so I had to close my eyes and exhale deeply before I addressed everything that was wrong with what she said. "Everything that girl just told you was a lie. Amber and I never had anything remotely close to a relationship. We never hung out, went on dates, none of that. The only time I hit her up was when I wanted to smash. It was only a sex thing between us. So why would I want a person I can't stand being around outside of sex to have a baby from me?" I asked, keeping it a stack with my mother. I didn't know whom I was more mad at: my mother for believing that bullshit or Amber's delusional ass for calling my mother with this shit. I was definitely done with her after this stunt that she'd pulled.

My mother's face softened. "Is it wrong for me to want my one and only child to experience love and happiness? I know I might be going about it the wrong way, but that's all the I want from you. Your father and I aren't going to be around forever, and I don't want to die knowing that you will be alone," she said with a lone tear rolling down her check that she wiped off. The anger I felt moments ago vanished when I saw tears coming from her eyes. I wasn't the most compassionate nigga, and many might say that I was heartless, but when it came to my mother, all that flew out the window. She was the only woman that could affect me with her tears.

I scooted over to her, wrapping my arms around her. When I felt like she had calm down, I positioned my body so I would be facing her. I grabbed both of her hands and placed them into to mine. "What you mean, you ain't gon' be around forever? You ain't getting away from me that easily. We are dying together," I joked, getting a laugh out of her. "But on a serious note, you don't have to worry about me, Ma. I'm good with being by myself right now. I have a lot of things going on that requires me to stay focused. I can't do that, being with someone. And you trying to hook me up with different women will not make me move any faster. But I promise you when the day comes that I decide to settle down with someone, you'll be the first to meet her, and if I get your stamp of approval, then I will give you as many grandkids as you want."

"I'm holding you to that," she said, pulling me into a hug.

After a few seconds, she released me from her embrace and stared at me. I could see the concern in her eyes, but honestly, she didn't have a reason to be. For as long as I could remember, she had been concerned with everyone else's well-being besides her own.

"Well, I'm about to head out of here to handle some business," I announced, standing up from the couch. "Do you need anything before I leave?"

She shook her head. "Did you see your father when you came in?" she asked.

"No, but his car is out front, so he gotta be in here somewhere."

"Okay. And don't forget about Sunday dinner. You have missed it for the last two weeks. If I don't see you tomorrow, I'm coming to your house and popping you upside your head," she threatened.

I laughed at my mother trying to sound hard. We both knew that she wasn't about that life. "Aight, gangsta, you ain't got to threaten me. I'll be here," I promised, heading out the room.

When I made it to my car, I scrolled through my contracts. Finding Amber's number, I waited until I heard her voice on the other line.

"Hey bab—"

Before she could finish her sentence, I cut her off. "I'm going to tell your silly ass this one time. Don't call my mama phone no-fucking-more on no fuck shit!" I roared. "Got her over here stressing out on some bullshit that your delusional ass made up. You will never be my bitch! Get that through your fucking head."

I heard her sniffling. "Why are you treating me like this? I love you. Why can't you see that those other bitches can't do half of the shit that I'm willing to do for you?" She cried through the phone.

I held the phone away from my ear because that loud ass crying she was doing was hurting my eardrums. "Contact anyone from my family again and see won't you be floating in a fucking river," I said before hanging up and blocking her number. I threw my phone in the passenger seat. Resting my head on the headrest, I closed my eyes, running both hands down my face before cranking up the car and pulling out of the driveway. *Fuck waiting until next month; I was going on vacation next week.*

# Sasha

I sat at the park on the bench, staring out at the wide-open space. I didn't care that it was forty-eight degrees and that every little move I made caused my body to shiver even though I was covered up from head to toe. I was sure that I was going to have a bad cold in the morning, but none of that mattered to me right now. Feeling defeated, I let the tears of frustration that I had been holding in fall freely down my face. I had spent my day going to art museums, trying to get art dealers to look at my pieces, but no one did.

Hell, I couldn't even show them my work before they said they weren't interested. Maybe I should give it up. It had been almost three years since I'd graduated, and I was still stuck in the same position. I guess people were right when they told me that having an art degree wasn't shit, and I wouldn't make any money from it. I should just wait until my lease was up and move back to Georgia and help my parents out with their auto shop business. It wasn't like I was doing anything in Texas with my life. Wiping the snot off my nose, I dug in the pocket of my coat to get my ringing phone. When I saw my mom's name on the screen, I cleared my throat, trying to sound as normal as I could.

"Hey, Mommy. How are you doing?" I asked cheerfully.

"I'm good. I'm in the middle of making dinner and decided to call you since I haven't heard from you in a few days."

"I talked to you two days ago," I responded, rolling my eyes at my mom's dramatics.

I could hear the sound of cabinets opening and closing. "Same difference. It was still a few days ago. Now tell me what's wrong with you. I can hear it in your voice that you've been crying," she said in a concerned voice.

"What you mean? I haven't been crying; my nose is just a little stuffy," I said, not wanting my mom to worry.

"Sasha Nicole Braley, I have been your mother for the past twenty-three years, so I know when something is wrong with my child. You either tell me now, or I'll schedule a trip to Texas to find out for myself."

I broke down again. "This past year, I have been to at least fifty art dealers, but not one of them would even take the time to even look at my paintings. I feel like I should just give up and come back home." I cried.

"Oh, Sasha, it's going to be okay. Just continue doing what you are doing, and it's going to pay off," I heard her say, but I didn't believe it.

"You are always telling me that, and it has yet to happen."

"Now, I know that you might not want to hear this, but because it's not your time. You have to struggle a little to appreciate your success. Anyone can tell that you have the talent to become big, but if you are going to just give up and run back home, then baby, you are going to be running for the rest of your life. Everyone wants to be an overnight success but don't take into consideration the work that comes along with it. It's going to be times where you want to give up, but the goal is to keep going. Do you understand me?"

"Yes, ma'am."

"But if you feel like you need to come back home and get yourself together, that's fine. I just want you to know that your father and I walk around the house naked, so if you think you can—"

I couldn't let her finish that sentence. "Eww, Mommy, that's nasty. I could've lived my life without knowing what that." I didn't even want to think of my parents still getting it in. That was too much for me.

"Well, that's what you have to look forward to if you chose to come back," she said, laughing. "Whatever you chose to do, then I'll support. Just don't give up on something that you love to do, okay? Now I'm about to finish up with the dinner, and I'll call and check up on you later on tonight before I go to sleep, and you better answer your phone."

"I will, and tell Dad I said hey when he makes it in from work."

We said our goodbyes and ended the call. I cleaned off the remainder of my tears with the back of my hands and made my way to my car. I felt a little better than I originally was after talking to my mother. Once inside, I turned the heat on full blast. I placed my hands on top of the vents so they could warm up before I pulled off. While driving, I felt my stomach growl, reminding me that I hadn't eaten all day. Since I was down the street from Subway, I decided to pick something up before heading home.

I was happy that the place only had a handful of people. I walked up to the counter and placed my order. As I was about to pay for my food, I felt a tap on my shoulder. I turned around and got the surprise of my life when I saw Shawn, a dude I was cool with in high school, but he looked different now. He was no longer the nerdy, lanky boy that had a face full of acne and buck teeth and wore square glasses that were too big for his face. This version of Shawn looked like a whole meal. Even though he was still lanky, he had a little meat on him, rocking a low haircut with waves that were making me seasick. He no longer wore glasses, and he had braces, and his dark-chocolate skin was now blemish free.

"Are you going to give me a hug or stare at me all day?" he asked, wearing a smile on his face.

Snapping back to reality, I gave him a hug. "I haven't seen you in years. What are you doing here? Last I heard, you were doing undergrad at Hampton."

Aside from his looks, I was genuinely happy to see him. We were really close in high school. He was my guy best friend. When I first saw him, he was sitting at a table by himself, eating lunch alone. I saw the sad look that he wore while he was looking around at everyone socializing with each other, and it tugged at my heart. I rarely approached a person first, but I knew the feeling of being an outcast, so I walked over to the table he was sitting at, not saying a word, just eating. I did this for a week straight until he finally spoke to me. After that day, we became good friends.

Shawn was the definition of 'don't judge a book by its cover.' His appearance wasn't much back then, but he was the kindest, sweetest, smartest person I'd ever came across to this day. After graduating, we still kept in contact until the end of freshmen year. Even though we stopped talking to each other, my mom and his mom were still friends, so when I had heard from my mother that he was planning on proposing to his then girlfriend, I was hurt a little. It didn't have anything to do with me having feelings for him or anything like that, but I thought I would be the first person to know since we were close. After learning this information, I started to distance myself from him. I didn't want to cause problems in their relationship, so I started to talk to him less and less. After a couple of months went by, the commutation between us was pretty much non-existent.

"Yeah, I finished that up last year. I'm in Texas, visiting my mom's side of the family, but you would've known that already had you not dropped me like a call," he teased, causing me to laugh.

Before I could address what he'd said, the cashier cleared her throat. "I'm sorry to interrupt y'all conversation, but there are other customers waiting to get rung up," the cashier that looked like she was still in high school said in a sweet tone.

"I'm sorry," I apologized, taking out my wallet to pay, but before I could get the money out, Shawn was already handing her a twenty-dollar bill. I opened my mouth to decline, but he shook his head, signaling that he didn't want to hear my objection while receiving his change.

Even though I originally planned to get some food and head straight home, I decided that I could spend some time catching up with Shawn. "So how have you been for the last couple of years? And don't leave out any details either. Inquiring minds want to know."

"That's a very broad question, Sasha. I can't think of every single thing that I've done over the years. I'm an open book, so just tell me what you want to know, then I'll answer," he stated, making himself comfortable in the hard, wooden seats.

I playfully looked to the ceiling with my thumb and index finger on my chin. "Let's start with where you live now, and make our way from there."

"I live in New York, but I've been contemplating on moving back to Georgia or maybe Florida. I didn't realize how much I appreciated warm weather until moving to the East. I thought I was going to freeze to death my first year there." He laughed, giving me a glimpse of his blue-colored braces. I knew most adults would be against wearing colored braces or just braces in general, but with him, it just added on to his cuteness.

"I think you are overexaggerating. It can't be that bad. So paint a picture for me. Tell me what I would expect if I went there. I do want to know if it's all what it's cracked up to be," I said curiously.

"I can't necessarily 'paint a picture for you,'" he said, using air quotes. "I mean, it's way different from home, if that's what you are asking. Besides the cold weather, it's fast paced, the cost of living is high, and traffic is terrible, but you'll learn or see something new every day. It has so much culture there, and I'm not just talking about the different races of people. There's plenty of art, whether it's drawing, dancing, or rapping." I could tell he really loved living there; just hearing the passion in his voice as he spoke was a clear indication.

"So what is it that you do there?"

"I started off working for a big company that I had an internship with while I was in college where I advertised and designed websites. The money and benefits were good, but I wasn't happy there. I was constantly getting looked over even though I knew my ideas was better than the ones that was being chosen. After my first year of being there and seeing how they operated, I made up my mind that once I saved up enough money, I would quit. About two years later, I did just that. I eventually started up my own small business. It was a rough first couple of months, but business started picking up; now, a year later, I have companies that pay me top dollar to work with them, and the best part is I work from home."

"I'm so proud of you!" I squealed, reaching my arms around the table, giving him another hug. "You are just winning all around. Got your own business, and you have your Kofi Siriboe thing going for you, looking like a whole snack out in these streets," I playfully teased, pinching his jaw softly.

"A snack?" He looked offended. "Don't play yourself. I'm a full meal with dessert on the side." He brushed his hands on both side of his face, licking his lips before biting them. The shy, nerdy boy was now long gone. The person that sat in front of me was now a confident man.

I rolled my eyes. "Since you are a self-proclaimed meal with a dessert on the side, I know someone had the privilege to snatch you up? My momma told me that you were engaged to someone, but I notice that you aren't wearing a wedding ring, so I take it you didn't go through with it?" I inquired. I wasn't trying to be nosy. I had noticed that he didn't have a ring on his finger when we first sat down at the table, and I didn't want to lead the conversation with that being my first question.

"I see you have been checking up on me." He smirked, sitting up straight up in his chair.

"Don't flatter yourself. I didn't bring you up in conversation; she did. You know she always looked at you like her second child."

"That she did. I need to call and check up on her since I haven't done it in a while. I already know that she is going to curse my ass out as soon as she hears my voice, but to answer your question, I ended up calling off the engagement once I saw what type of person she really was. I knew I couldn't spend the rest of my life with someone like that," he said with a grim look on his face. I knew it had to be a painful reason for him not getting married.

I was just about to open my mouth to ask when his phone started to ring. He lifted his index finger, signaling for me to hold on so he could answer. He got up from the table, walking off. I figured that it was probably an important call and that it might be a while before he got off, so I grabbed my phone from inside my purse so I could see if anyone had called or texted me. Tori had texted me five minutes ago.

*Tori: Tell me why Justin stupid ass didn't come home last night and had the nerves to stroll in this morning like it was all good? I had to pray because I was so tempted to go upstairs to get my gun so I could kill his ass.*

*Me: You do realize that this man doesn't have a regular 9 to 5 type job. Shouldn't you be use to that anyways? I've stayed at your house a lot of times and he has did that so what's the difference now?*

*Tori: The difference is he usually called and told me he wasn't going to make it home, but last night I didn't get no call, text, shout, or anything. Hell, I didn't even get a SOS. Had me worried for no goddamn reason. I should cut his fine ass for that.*

**Me:** *LMAO... you are the only person I know that would curse and compliment your dude at the same time.*

**Tori:** *I may be mad at him, but that doesn't take away from him looking sexy as fuck. I give props where props are due. Any who, since I can't physically harm his ass, I'm just going to be petty and not come home tonight. I'm staying at your house so have my side of the bed ready. Lol*

**Me:** *Oh hell nawl! Y'all ain't about to turn my apartment into a war zone. You better stay at one of these expensive ass hotels and call it a day.*

**Tori:** *I'll be headed there as soon as I get off of work... kisses*

**Me:** *I'm not playing!*

I waited for her to respond back, but she never did. I was so serious. They weren't about to tear up my house behind something foolish. The last time Tori and Justin got into it, I ended up with a broken door, a big hole in the wall, and the landlord threatening to kick me out for disturbing the peace.

I saw Shawn walking back to the table. I placed my phone back in my purse so I could give him my undivided attention until I noticed that he was still standing.

"I'm sorry to cut this visit short, but I have something that I need to take care of right now. Give me your number so we can keep in contact," he said, handing me his phone. I typed and saved my number before returning it back to him.

"You do know that I'm going to pay you back, right?" I asked, gathering my sub and purse before standing up.

"I see nothing has changed with you." He chuckled. Damn, even that sounded good now. "But I know how you get, so I'll make you a deal. You can pay me back by spending the day with me before I head back home. It won't be considered as a date, just two friends catching up on old times. I wouldn't want you and your man beefing over a misunderstanding," he said, trying to pry for information.

"You don't have anything to worry about. I'm single as a dollar bill." I giggled.

"Okay, I was just making sure. Let me walk you to your car."

He followed me out the door to my car. He grabbed my keys, unlocking the door and opening the driver's side, waiting for me to get in before he closed it. I almost forgot how much of a gentleman he was.

"Be safe," he called out as I put my car in drive. I waved at him through the window as I pulled out the parking lot.

*****

I was laid out on my couch with my warm blue blanket covering up my body, trying to focus on the movie that was currently on the TV screen, but Tori's loud-mouthed ass was talking so much 'til I had to grab the remote and turn up the volume. I'd been trying to watch this movie for the past thirty minutes, but all I could hear was Tori boasting about Justin calling her back to back. As soon as I placed the remote beside my legs, I felt an object connect with the back of my head. Touching my head, I looked down and saw the spoon that Tori was eating her ice-cream with on the floor next to me. I slowly moved my eyes from the floor to Tori's face, mean mugging her.

"Why you being all rude and shit, turning this damn TV up so loud when I'm trying to talk to you?" she asked, returning the same facial expression.

"Because you've been talking about the same damn thing for that past half hour. Okay, Justin keeps calling you; that's what he always does when you aren't at home, and I'm pretty sure that he will be over here to carry your ass out before the night ends. Once y'all get home, it's going to be a fight, he'll fuck you senseless, and then you'll forgive him. I don't need to constantly hear about a story I already know the ending to," I said with a hint of aggravation, turning my back to her so I could try to get into the movie. I loved my cousin and all, but I didn't feel like hearing about her drama right now, especially when it was over something so petty. I had enough negativity surrounding me, and I didn't think I could handle anymore tonight. I just wanted to have a quiet night in the house, curl up, and watch a good movie.

"Damn, tell me how you really feel. Who pissed in your cereal this morning?" I heard her ask, but I didn't respond. "I know when I'm not wanted. I'm going to your room to sleep, and you better not wake me up either, or we gon' throw them hands, with your rude ass."

I could see her from my peripheral as she stomped to the back. She slammed the door, and I just shrugged my shoulders, snuggling up with my blanket so I could enjoy what was left of the movie. I was used to her tactics, and they didn't faze me one bit.

I was in the process of going to sleep when I heard my phone ringing near my ear. With my eyes still half closed, I tapped the screen and placed it to my ear. "Hello?" I answered in a groggy voice.

"Why are you showing me your damn ear?" the other person on the line said. My eyes popped open when I recognized who the voice it belonged to. I removed the phone from my ear and realized that instead of Ron calling, he had FaceTimed me. I shot my arm down so he wouldn't be able to see me anymore, and I felt myself beginning to panic a little. My heartrate increased, and my palms started to sweat. How did I not hear the difference in the ringtones? I knew I looked a mess when he saw my face. I no longer had the box braids, so my hair was in a sloppy, bushy ball on the top my head. I had a little bit of drool coming out the corner of my mouth, and my lips felt dry and crusty.

"Um… can you hold a second? I'll be back," I said, nearly running to the bathroom. I grabbed my brush and edge control so I could fix my edges a little. Every woman with natural hair knew the importance of laying your edges. A woman could be having a bad hair day, but as soon as she did those edges, she would be good to go. Taking off the elastic wrap that held my hair in the ball together, I put some edge control on and smoothed my hair back before placing my thick curls back into a ball. I wasn't into giving myself baby hairs. I felt like if you didn't have it in your adulthood, what's the point of making some? But to each its own. I got some Vaseline from under the bathroom counter and rubbed it on my lips. Once I saw that I was presentable enough, I walked back to the living room, put the television on mute, and covered my lower half with my blanket before I picked my phone up, looking at the screen.

"I'm bac—" My words got stuck in my throat when I saw Ron's handsome face.

His eyes were hooded to the point I couldn't really see the color of them. From that alone, I could tell that he had been smoking. Also, he was lying in bed with no shirt on, displaying his six-pack. I was pleasantly surprised to see that he didn't have any tattoos on his chest, stomach, or arms. He looked and acted like the type that would have them on every inch of his body. *Maybe he had some on his back or legs,* I wondered.

"It's about time. I started to hang up on yo' ass. I see that you went and fixed yourself up a little for me." He smiled lazily.

Instead of acknowledging what he said, I redirected the conversation. "I'm surprised that you took the time out of your busy day to talk to me, but what made you FaceTime me? You don't strike me as the type to do this," I said, referring to the FaceTime call.

"I don't, but you were on my mind. I wanted to check up on you and see if you were good. I haven't seen or spoken to you since that day you basically threw my ass out of your apartment."

I felt bad a little. I knew, in his own way, he was trying to see what was wrong with me, but I didn't feel like talking about it. However, that still didn't give him the right to snap on me the way that he did. "I'm good. It was just one of those days, you know," I replied, not wanting to give any further details.

He nodded his head in response. "I feel ya. It be like that sometimes.

A comfortable silence lingered between us until I spoke again. "I notice that we have been texting back and forth for a while, but I still know little to nothing about you on a deep level. Why is that?" I gave him a curious stare.

I watched him as he scratched the top of his head. "The same reason I don't know shit about you," he shot back with a sly smirk.

"I'm curious to know what reason that might be, sir." I positioned my body so I could rest my head on a couch pillow since sitting up was starting to make my back ache.

"Because we don't know each other well enough to disclose personal information like that. Don't get me wrong; you are a cool ass person to converse with when you ain't throwing out slick comments, but in order for me to trust someone with information like that, I'd have to be around them to get a sense of what type of person they really are, and since I'm always busy as fuck, I don't see that happening, not unless you make time around your schedule to accommodate mine," he said matter-of-factly.

"So you are telling me that the only way I'll know anything of importance about you is if I wait on you to hit me up saying you want to see me?" I frowned my face up. I had to be sure that was what he was saying before I went off on him.

He shook his head. "No, I'm saying that I don't have a regular work schedule like these other niggas do. I work around the clock, and most days, I usually don't step foot in my house until sunrise. So unless you woke up earlier than you normally do just to meet me somewhere or catch me on one of my slow days, then I don't see us chilling no time soon."

"You ever heard of the phrase 'people make time for who they want to make time for'?"

"That applies to regular niggas, not me. I'm in a league of my own. Remember that." He cockily winked at me. "What type of panties you got on? Better yet, move your phone down so I can see for myself."

I threw my head back in laughter. "You are funny, you know that? Not even two minutes ago, you gave this little speech about how you weren't willing to become personal with me, but you want to see what type of panties I'm wearing like that's not personal? You are set tripping, dude."

"Set tripping?" he asked, his face laced with confusion. "What the hell does that mean?"

Before I could respond, I heard banging at my door. I already knew that it was Justin coming to get Tori, so I went to unlock the door, not bothering to look back, allowing him access in.

"Where is your petty ass cousin at!" he barked as soon as he stepped into the house. I pointed to the back, getting into the same spot I was before he came banging at the door. Justin rushed to the room, and I instantly heard screaming.

"Damn, who doing all that fucking screaming?" Ron asked when he saw my face on the screen again.

"Tori was planning on spending the night over here, but your friend just popped up over here to take her back to their house, and as you can hear, it's not going too well." I sighed, shaking my head. With all the screaming they were doing, I was positive that some of my neighbors were pissed off.

"I'm not even surprised by that shit. Their asses are always arguing. I couldn't deal with that shit. It'll have me ready to choke her ass."

"You hit women?" I asked, giving him the side eye.

"Nawl, but I have yoked up a couple of bitches that wanted to be bad and show out. If I ever hit a woman, my mama would kill my ass, but I'm not going to say I haven't thought about it once or twice."

I looked up just in time to see Justin carrying Tori across his shoulder while she hit him in the back with her dreads swinging wildly across her head.

"Put me down, or I promise, I will bite the shit out your shoulder!" she screamed at him.

"Do that shit, and I will throw yo' ass down these stairs. Play with it if you want to," he threatened her in a deadly tone. She looked at me for help, but I turned my head away. If I felt like he would harm her, then I'd help, but I knew that he wouldn't. Plus, I had been learned not to get involved in their relationship.

"Aye, Sasha, we about to go. Lock up." He stopped in mid-step. "Wait. Hold up. Is that my nigga Ron I see on the phone, caking up and shit?" Justin asked, looking toward my phone screen. His once cold voice was replaced by a teasing one.

"Fuck you," Ron spat.

"Don't get mad that you got caught, my nigga, but I'mma holla at you tomorrow. As you can see, I got a situation that needs to be taken care," he said opening the door.

"Nigga, you ain't gon' take care of sh—Ow! Motherfucker, that hurt!" Tori shouted. Justin had smacked her hard as hell on the ass.

"Shut that shit up before I do it again. Got me out in the middle of the night coming to find you. Do some stupid shit like this again, and I'm chaining you up to the bed and not like how your freaky ass like it either," he said, walking out the door.

I closed and locked the door behind me before cutting off the TV and lights, heading to my bedroom with my phone in hand. I got in bed, placing my head on my pillow. I turned the phone sideways so I could see his face. I noticed that he had a serious look on his face.

"What are you over there thinking about that got you looking so serious?" I inquired.

"I'm thinking about what it would feel having you face down, moaning my name while I'm digging in your guts from the back."

My eyes widened with shock.

"I got your ass speechless, huh?" he asked, licking his lips before he bit them. I had to squeeze my legs together to try and stop my vagina from throbbing. "I will bet money that your pussy is leaking at this very moment."

"Boy, bye. You must didn't comprehended when I said that my vagina has standards, and you don't meet any of them?" I responded, trying to play off the fact that he was right.

He chuckled. "I find it funny that you would bring that up. If that lame ass nigga that I saw at the mall with you that day got you to pop that pussy for him, then you are right. I don't meet your standards, because they are low as fuck. Word of advice, baby girl, if you are going to entertain a nigga, make sure his ass ain't a habitual pill popper," he let me know.

"What did you just say?" I had to hear it again. I knew he didn't just say that Kendrick popped pills.

"You heard what the fuck I just said. Ole dude that had you hemmed up at the mall pop pills like it's candy. I've seen him multiple times around the way buying that shit, but if that's the type of nigga that gets your pussy wet, then that's on you," he said, dropping a bomb on me.

I was at a loss for words. Kendrick was a pill head? It was starting to all make sense now. I knew that he had been acting different for a while, but I just thought it was stress from him job or something of that nature. I momentarily went back in my memory, trying to pinpoint exactly when I first noticed the difference, but I just came up blank. That would also explain why he was so aggressive that day at the mall.

"From that dumb look on your face, I can tell that you didn't know he was into that shit."

"No, I didn't," I replied in a tone just above a whisper. I was still in shock of the information that he just dropped on me.

"Don't be too hard on yourself. It's a lot of niggas out here that hide that shit. You just happened to get caught up with one, but enough about that shit. I have a proposition for you."

I didn't like the way he said that. It sounded like something that a pimp would tell a girl that he was trying to get to hoe for him. "What is it?" I asked with a skeptical look.

"I'm going out of town this weekend, and I want you to join me, and before you get excited, it ain't on no 'I'm trying to be with you' type shit either. I can tell that you need to get away just from the look in your eyes, and I can help you with that. Plus, I'm still trying to figure out something."

I looked at his face, trying to find any small indication that he was joking. Surely, he had to be. This was the same man that just said that we didn't know each other like that, but here he was, asking me to go on an out-of-town trip with him. "Are you serious?"

"Yeah, I'm dead ass. Something you have to learn about me is that I rarely play about shit. If I open my mouth to tell you something, don't question it. Now are you rolling or not?" he asked with a stoned face.

I started weighing the pros and cons in my head. I did need an escape from Texas, even if it was just the weekend, but I didn't know this man well enough to go somewhere out of the state with him. He'd already shown me that he had a limited amount of patience when it came to people, and he was easily angered. If I said one wrong thing to him, I was quite sure I would be on the ten o'clock news with 'have you seen her' typed above my picture. I would have to get Tori's advice on this.

I didn't want to say no, but I didn't want to say yes just yet either without getting a second opinion. "Can I get back to you on that?" I responded.

He blew out a sigh of frustration. "I'm giving you two days. And I'm not about to run up behind yo' ass just to get one. If I don't have an answer by then, it's your loss. I have never even asked a woman to go out and about with me, let alone go on a trip. You should feel privileged that I'm willing to bless you with my time. Do you know how many bitches wish I would ask them to go someplace with them?"

"I can only imagine," I replied sarcastically while rolling my eyes.

"Keep rolling the bitches, and one day, they gon' get stuck. You gon' be walking around here looking like Musiq Soulchild; eyes gon' be cock like a motherfucker. You gon' have to wear sunglasses just so a person will know that you are talking to them and not the person on the other side."

I was laughing so hard that my stomach started to tighten up, and my back began to hurt. "You know you are foul for that," I said in between laughter.

"I just tell it how it is. Don't get me wrong. The nigga can sing his ass off, but his eyes do look like they are throwing up a gang sign."

"I am so done with you right now, Ron," I said, wiping the tears in the corner of my eyes.

"Aye, but look, I'mma have to get up with you later. I have to be up in a few hours, so I'm about to take my black ass to sleep before I be ready to body any nigga that even sneeze too loud. Let's just say I'm not a very reasonable person if I don't at least get four hours of sleep."

"The real question is when are you ever a reasonable person?"

"When I want to be. Now get the fuck off my line," he said before ending the call.

I put my phone on the charger beside me. I grabbed my purple bonnet that was on my nightstand and placed it on my head before lying back down, staring at the ceiling. Even though it was nearly four in the morning, oddly, I wasn't sleepy or tired anymore. I was glad that it was still the weekend, and I didn't have to go to work. I knew if I did, I would pay dearly.

My thoughts wandered to Kendrick. I was still confused about how I didn't know the signs before. I wondered if he started popping pills around the same time people started telling me about him cheating on me. I wondered what caused him to even start doing that in the first place when I knew for a fact that wasn't his thing. When he and I first started talking, he didn't do drugs. He barely touched alcohol. That was one amongst several things we had in common. I shook off the thought of him. I still cared about his well-being, and I prayed that he got the help that he needed to kick his habit, but he was no longer my problem.

A smile crept on my face with the thought of spending the weekend away with Ron. I was getting butterflies now in my stomach just thinking about it. My mother always told me that if you fought the truth, it would start making you look older. I had to stop lying to myself like I wasn't feeling this man when I knew that I was, but why? He was the polar opposite of everything that I went for in a guy, including his looks.

I was attracted to cute dudes that were funny, sweet, and calm natured, but Ron was sexy, and the bad part was that he knew it. With his looks and sex appeal, he could have women doing any and everything for him, down to stealing from their own mother if he asked them to. He had an attitude problem, and I got the sense that aside from his family, he didn't take into consideration anybody's feelings, and he was anything but calm.

But I saw something else to him, though—more than an asshole with a cocky attitude and a terrible temper that he showed on the outside layer. Just like Shawn, it could be more to him than met the eye, and if I decided to take him up on his offer, hopefully, I'd get to see another side of him.

*****

"Well, if it isn't my fake ass cousin calling to finally check up on me after what? A whole twenty-five hours later," Tori said as soon as she picked up. I knew that she would have an attitude with me, but I had a peace offering for her.

"Hey to you too, Tori," I said politely, ignoring her sarcasm. "I'm down the street from your house, and I was wondering if you wanted any company?" I waited for her to answer, but the only thing I got was silence. "I have chocolate-covered strawberries and some wine."

"The door will be unlocked," I heard her say before she hung up. I smiled to myself. *Gets her every time,* I thought, driving to her house.

Once I made it, I opened the door and called her name. When she was responded that she was in her bedroom, I made my way up the stairs with the wine in one hand and the box of strawberries in the other. When I entered the room, she was sitting on the bed, slumped over, painting her toenails. She peered at me momentarily before rolling her eyes and continuing to paint her toes.

I stood in place, not sure of how I was going to get back in her good graces. "I have the wine and the strawberries," I said, waving them in my hands so she could see them, but she never looked up from what she was doing.

Seeing how Plan A didn't work out for me, I went to Plan B. I ran over to where she was and hopped on the bed with her. I wrapped my arms around her tightly so she wouldn't get out of my embrace. "I'm sorry for getting an attitude with you and not saying anything to Justin, so can you please stop being mad at me?" I begged.

I could feel her trying to wiggle away from me, but that only made me strengthen my arms around her body even more. "I'm not going to let go until you accept my apology."

"Okay, fine, I forgive you, so move. It's already burning up in here, and here you go, bringing your hot-body ass over here. If I would've fucked up and got this fingernail polish on my bed sheets, I was going to beat your ass and then make you pay for it. Now pass me that box of strawberries before I get mad again."

Smiling, I obliged her request. She stuffed her mouth with a strawberry, still paying attention to her feet. I decided to get to the real reason why I came over here in the first place.

"So I need your advice on something?"

"Mm hmm... I knew it was another reason why you came over here besides asking for my forgiveness. I'm listening."

"Ron asked me if I wanted to go out of town with him this weekend, and I wanted your opinion on if I should go," I said, nervously biting my lips.

She finished up her last nail before she finally responded. "That's something you have to figure out for yourself. I can't make that decision for you. I mean, do you want to go with him?"

I thought about it for a second. "I do."

"Okay, then what's the problem?"

"I don't want to go on this trip with a certain expectation and end up disappointed if it doesn't happen." I sighed. I'd finally come out and said what I had been feeling since he asked me the question. I knew that he said that it wouldn't be a couple's trip, but I wanted it to be.

Tori peered at me. "Do you want my honest opinion?"

I nodded my head in response.

"With the type of reputation Ron has, I would think the only reason that he asked you to go was to sleep with you, but then again, he ain't the type of nigga that has to pay for pussy, so it could be that he sees something in you. So if you want to go, then go. Have fun, especially since I'm sure you won't have to pay for anything, but if you feel like you shouldn't go, then you don't have to explain why you don't want to go. I don't know, but whatever the case may be, I don't think you should expect to be in a relationship once y'all return, but hey, I could be wrong."

I took in everything that she was telling me. I was having a debate with myself. I did want to go, but Tori unknowingly planted a seed in my head. *What if he only invited me to get in my pants?*

"Where are y'all supposed to be going anyway?" Tori asked me.

Just as I was about to open my mouth to reply, my phone started to vibrate in my back pocket. I held my hands up and looked on the screen, and Shawn's named appeared.

"Hey, what's up?" I said as soon as I answered.

"Nothing, I just wanted to see if you were available to hang out with me this weekend?" his smooth voice asked.

"Umm… I'm not sure. I might be busy this weekend. What about next weekend?" I was praying that he would agree because I still wanted to hang out with him so we could catch up with each other.

"That's cool with me, but just in case you want to cancel on me, I want to let you know that I'm leaving next month."

"You don't have to worry about that. I wouldn't do my best friend like that," I said, laughing. "But I'm having a conversation with my cousin right now. Can I call you later on tonight, if it's possible? Not unless you will be busy or something?"

"Oh, my bad. Yeah, we can. I won't be busy. Sorry for interrupting."

After we hung up, Tori wore an accusing look. "What?"

"So who was this *best friend* of yours that you plan to call later that got you smiling and shit?" she questioned.

"Do you remember Shawn that used to come back when you visited during the summer?"

She tilted her head to the side, tapping on her chin. "Shawn. Shawn. Shawn. Oh, you are talking about the socially awkward dude with the buck teeth, bifocal glasses, and a face full of acne. When did y'all start back talking?"

"He is in town. When I went to get something to eat a few days ago, he saw me, and we talked for a little while before exchanging numbers. And let me tell you, the glow up was real with him. He is sexy now. I mean like a Kofi sexy," I excitedly described him, right down to his braces.

"Well, damn. I have to see him for myself. If he looks as good as you say he does, then Justin might have some competition on his hands. You know how much I love Kofi, with his sexy, dark-chocolate ass. Shit, just thinking about him got me pulsating," she said, closing her eyes like she was envisioning him in her head. When she finally opened her eyes, she received a look of disgust from me. "I'm sorry, girl. You know how I get when someone mentions his name." She started fanning herself.

My phone started vibrating in my hands again. Ron's named appeared, and I automatically got nervous.

"If that's Shawn calling again, tell him to FaceTime you so that I can see if you were exaggerating or not."

"It's Ron. What should I say?" I panicked, feeling the butterflies surface.

"Tell him your decision. Da fuck?" she replied like it should've been obvious.

Waving her off, I took a deep breath before answering the call.

"Hello," I answered shyly.

"Let me know something," he said, referring to if I was going with him or not.

"I thought you said that you wouldn't call me—that I had to hit you up, or it would be my loss," I recited his words. "And why is your background so loud?

"Fuck all that shit that you are talking about, and tell me what's up. Is you rolling or not?"

I looked toward Tori for help, but she just shrugged her shoulders.

"I'm going," I finally responded after a minute of silence. I figured that if I went with Ron and it didn't end well, at least I wouldn't have to wonder what if.

I heard him talking to someone in the background, but I couldn't make out what was being said. "Aight. I'mma pull up at your apartment around seven Saturday morning. Have all your shit packed and ready to go. Don't have me waiting all day for you either."

"Okay."

"I'm in the middle of taking care of some business, so I'mma holla at you later."

"Wait!" I yelled before he could hang up. "You never told me where you are taking me."

He chuckled. "You'll find out when we get there," he said, hanging up.

I turned around facing Tori with a huge smile on my face. "Well, it looks like I'm going."

She rolled her eyes, smiling at me as well. "Yo' love-sick ass over there smiling like this nigga gave you the winning number to the Power Ball prize." We started laughing, but then her face grew serious. "Just be careful with him, OK? I know you aren't used to dealing with a man like Ron, and I don't want to see you hurt, because I just might kill him over you."

I could see the concern in her eyes and hear the worry in her voice. Even though I appreciated her willingness to protect me, she had to realize that I was a grown woman. I had to make my own mistakes in order for me to grow. She couldn't protect me from everything.

"I will," I promised, hugging her as she returned the gesture.

"Just to let you know, I will be sending you a list of Do's and Don'ts via text, so be expecting that," she said, sounding like my mother. "Now, enough with all this mushy shit. Let's drink this wine and watch a movie or two before you leave. I made some tacos today."

After hearing her say tacos, I rushed downstairs to retrieve some. I stuffed my plates with four soft-shelled tacos with a bunch of sour cream on the side and a bottle of water before I went back upstairs to enjoy the rest of my visit.

*****

I had been losing sleep over for the past four days. I stayed up half the night, packing. I would've finished earlier, but since I didn't know exactly where we were going, I had a hard time choosing outfits and shoe wear. I didn't know if I needed to dress down or up. I texted Ron multiple times, trying to see if he would tell me, but the only response I kept getting from him was *you'll know when we get there.* After going back and forth with myself, I decided to dress in what I felt comfortable wearing. I paced back and forth in my living room, mentally going over the list in my head to make sure I had everything that I would need. I looked at my phone to see what time it was. It was 6:50 a.m. I still had a little time to make myself a smoothie to hopefully give me a boost of energy and to calm my nerves down.

As soon as I finished pouring the last of the mixture into my drinking container, I heard a hard knock on the door. I ran my hands over my hair and clothes, making sure everything was in place before I finally opened the door, and my eyes beheld a beautiful sight. Ron was leaning against the wall near the door, rolling around the toothpick that was in his mouth. I wasn't sure if I was imaging things, but it seemed as if his hazel eyes had lightened even more. His hair was pulled into a low ponytail with a red snapback covering his head. A plain red hoodie fitted loosely on him, washed jeans hung slightly off his hip, and a pair of all white Jordans were on his feet. The only jewelry that he had on was a diamond chain and a Rolex on his arm.

I'd been picked up on the fact that Ron wasn't the flashy type like most of these dudes that had money. I never saw him wear a gang of unnecessary jewelry or expensive designer clothing, even though I was pretty sure he owned a bunch of them. I could tell that he would rather be low-key and not have all the attention on him, but I knew that would be difficult, seeing as how he had the aura of a boss surrounding him. If he spoke, I was positive that anyone in hearing distance would listen.

I saw his tongue move across his lips as his eyes roamed over my body. A smug grin spread across his face while he eyed me lustfully, nodding his head in approval.

"You are looking good, baby girl, and I see you trying to match my fly." He smiled at me, showing his perfect pearly white teeth.

It hadn't dawned on me that we were wearing similar outfits until he mentioned it. I was wearing a white crop-top hoodie that showed a small amount of my toned stomach, red high-waist distress jeans that hugged the little butt that I had, and a pair of white Chuck Taylors on my feet. My hair was in a smooth, low puff with a part on the side, and a pair of big silver hoops decorated my ear.

"This was purely a coincidence. It wasn't like I was looking through your bedroom window just to see what you would wear. You ever heard of *great minds think alike?*"

"I see yo' little ass already starting off with that slick ass mouth. Keep talking, and I'mma give you something to shut that ass up." He smirked, biting his pink, kissable lips. "Is this what you bringing?" he asked, pointing to my blue and pink suitcase and my blue bag that held my all my necessities that were located by the by the door.

"Yeah."

He picked up both my suitcase and bag, walking out the door. I grabbed my smoothie, along with a straw and my purse, before locking the door behind us. Once in the car, no words were spoken between us. Only the sounds of the latest rap songs could be heard playing throughout the car, but I didn't mind one bit. I was nervous to the point I couldn't sit still and kept having to switch hands to hold my cup because my palms were sweating badly.

"Why do you keep moving? Are you cold or som'? I can turn up the heat a little bit more if you want," Ron said, looking between the road and me.

"No, I'm good. I'm just nervous I guess," I admitted.

"Nervous? Why? I'm not going to bite you or no shit like that. I'm just a regular ass person."

"That's easy for you to say because you are you. You don't know what it's like being around you, let alone trying to talk to you. It's this intimidating demeanor that you possess that makes me nervous," I said. *And the fact that I like you doesn't help my anxiety either.*

"I'm just a regular ass nigga. If I allow you in my space, I want you to feel comfortable being around me. So tell me what I can do for you to feel more relaxed. I can't have you being stiff and on mute this entire trip. You're gonna have people thinking that I kidnapped you or some shit like that." He smiled, gently pinching my cheek. I blushed.

"Okay, let's play twenty questions. I ask you something, you have to answer, and vice versa."

"That's cool, but I have one rule. Don't try to use this game to get any deep shit out of me. If I want to tell you anything on that level, it'll be on my own accord," he told me in a serious voice.

I wanted to protest, but then I realized he had a point. I would just wait and let him open up to me on his own time.

"Okay, fair enough. Um… let me see. What's your favorite food?" I started off.

"Pasta. What size clothes do you wear?

I looked at him with a frown. "Your mama never told you not to ask a woman her age, weight, and size?"

"Yeah, but only for people that look old as hell and fat. You don't fall into either of those boxes, so I figured that you wouldn't care if I asked."

"An extra small in shirts, and a two in jeans, sometimes a three on a good day." I groaned, really not wanting to answer. We spent the next twenty minutes going back and forth, asking questions to one another. I realized through the game that we liked a lot of the same things. We had the same taste in music, sports, and clothes.

Noticing that he was pulling the car up to an airport, I gazed at him, looking for an explanation. "Why are we at an airport? I thought that this was supposed to be like a road trip or something of that nature."

He didn't say anything, only killing the engine and opening the door to retrieve our things. I followed behind him, wondering what he had planned up his sleeves.

I watched as an old handsome Spanish man with reddish looking hair approached Ron and grabbed our luggage from out of his hands.

"Hello, Mr. Carson. How are you doing on this lovely morning?" he asked with a warm smile.

"Lovely morning? I can tell that you are getting old, Joe. It's cold as hell out here," Ron said, embracing the older man I now knew as Joe. "How are the wife and kids?"

"They are all doing well. My son made the honor roll again, and my daughter is preparing for college. The wife and I will be celebrating our anniversary in a couple of weeks, and I'm thinking about taking her back to our home country in Cuba for a few days."

"You are always welcome to use the jet anytime you are ready to leave," Ron offered.

I stood in the background, watching how these two interacted with one another. I could tell from their friendly demeanor that they shared a close relationship.

"And who might this beautiful young lady be?" Joe asked Ron, smiling in my direction.

"Oh, my bad. Joe, this is Sasha. Sasha, this is Joe," he introduced us. Joe extended his hand toward me, and I shook it. Joe had such an infectious smile that I couldn't help but smile right along with him.

"All this time I've worked for Mr. Carson, he has never brought someone on a trip. You must be a special person to him." He gave me a look that I couldn't quite make out.

"Cut all that out, and stop putting my business out here. She is just somebody I'm trying to get to know if she stop acting so damn scared around me," he said, looking over his shoulders at me.

Rolling my eyes, I fought the urge to stick my middle finger up at him.

"Make sure you treat her right. I can tell this one right here is a keeper. I've lived long enough to know a good woman when I see one," he said to Ron before addressing me. "You will have to excuse his mouth in advance. He says a lot of reckless things, but he is a good kid at heart," Joe advised.

"Enough with all that shit." Ron grabbed my hand, pulling me toward his private jet. "It was nice talking to you, Joe. Send the family my love, and before I forget, my mom says she has a bone to pick with you for not showing up to the event she hosted last week," he called out over his shoulder.

"Will do, and I'll personally apologize to her myself. Enjoy your stay in Hawaii."

"Hawaii!" I yelled.

*****

I woke up to Ron shaking me gently. I looked around, rubbing the little bit of drool I had on the corner of my mouth. I had fallen asleep four hours within the plane leaving the airport. I was a nervous wreck once we hit the sky. I'd never rode a plane before, and I was scared shitless. I Googled on my phone how long it would take to get there, and I almost lost it when I read almost seven hours. Ron tried to calm me down by pulling me close to him, but that didn't do anything. Once he saw that it wasn't working, he asked me if I wanted something to drink to help me out, and I told him yes.

After four glasses of wine, I was done. I wasn't a drinker, so any small amount of alcohol would have me tipsy, and unlike some people, once I got tipsy, I didn't fuss, fight, yell, or act out of character. I fell asleep.

It was sunny when we stepped off the plane. The Hawaiian sun beat down on my skin, warming and basking my arms in its radiance. A burst of warm air greeted me, and I closed my eyes, welcoming it. The air felt wonderful here. The breeze was blowing, and I felt a little mist, causing me to feel as if my skin was getting a light kiss. I couldn't believe it! I was actually in Hawaii.

I heard Ron calling my name, pulling me out of my trance. He was standing next to a black limo that I assumed was there to pick us up. Opening the door, the driver greeted us before picking up our things and putting them in the truck. Once he pulled off, I couldn't help but stare out the window in awe. I had to roll down the window to really enjoy the view. This was one of the most beautiful places that

I'd been. It just seemed as if everything was so peaceful here. I took my iPhone out, taking pictures of the scenery so I could send them to Tori and my mother. I rolled the window back up and laid my head back, wearing a grin. This was definitely a sign I'd made the right decision to come.

"With the way you are over there taking pictures of everything that you see, I take it yo' overly happy ass never been here before?"

I looked over in his direction. "No, I haven't. Thank you for bringing me here. I always wanted to visit but never had the chance to. I was supposed to go for my high school graduation along with Tori and her sister, but my dad got admitted into the hospital the day before we planned to leave because his blood pressure had gotten so high that he almost ended up in a coma. So we had to cancel the trip. I wasn't tripping, though. I preferred being there for my dad, making sure that he was okay, rather than going on the trip and constantly worrying if he would be okay."

"I'm sorry to hear that, but I'm glad I thought to bring you with me. You can't ever say that I'm an asshole now."

"Yes I can. Just because I'm getting the nicer side of you right now doesn't mean before the day is over with, your asshole side won't emerge. Can I ask you something?"

He nodded his head.

"Why did you bring me with you? I mean, I know you said it was due to the fact that it looked like I needed an escape for a while, which is true, but I just wanted to know if that was the only reason," I asked nervously, playing with my nails. I was silently wishing that the reason was that he felt the same way I was feeling about him.

He stared at me with a look so intense that it had me a little shook. "You ask too many questions. Just chill and enjoy the ride," was his only response.

After a while of riding with me getting excited over everything I saw, the limo pulled in front of the resort where we would be staying for the entire trip. I was at a loss for words. The resort was nothing short of spectacular. There were a bunch of trees and red flower bushes with small ponds that held clear blue water alongside the walkway into the entrance.

The driver opened the door so we could get out the limo. Ron held out his hand, and I gladly took it. We walked with our hands intertwined with one another all the way to the front desk where Ron signed in, getting our keys for the room. I noticed that he had only one key, and I wondered if he planned for us to sleep in the same room together. Taking the elevator, we finally made it to our floor. I followed Ron as he looked for the room that held our number. When we walked in the room, the only thing I could say was, "Wow."

It was a two-bedroom suite that had an ocean view. This room was literally almost the size of my apartment back home. Also, I was relieved that even though we were in the same room, we had our own bedrooms. I walked into the living room area, placing my things by the sofa. Looking out the screen doors, I saw that this room also came with a balcony. I ran out to get a closer look, and my eyes roamed over the resort, then they focused on the ocean. It was so calming to gaze at. Mentally, I told myself that I was coming back out here later to this breathtaking view. I walked back inside and saw Ron stretched out across the sofa, looking at something on his phone.

"Which bedroom will I sleep in?" I questioned, picking up my things.

"The one to the right, but you are more than welcome to join me in my room. You might get scared during the night and need someone that will protect you. Don't worry. I won't bite," he said to me with lust-filled eyes, running his tongue across his lips. And just like that, my hormones were starting to surface while I stood frozen. "Calm your scary ass down. I was just playing." He burst out laughing.

"Wh-what are you talking about? I didn't take you serious anyways, but just in case you were, I live by myself. If I find myself getting scared, I'll just turn on the TV, but thanks for the offer," I said, heading in the direction of where I would be sleeping at tonight, annoyed at myself for letting him see that he had gotten to me again. Throwing my things on the bed, I unzipped my suitcase and got out a pair of black leggings and a sports bra so I could take a shower and wash the plane scent off. After I had finished up, my body flopped on the bed. The silk sheets felt good brushing against my skin. I let out a big yawn. I was still a little sleepy even though I had taken a nap on the jet. Grabbing my phone, I set an alarm to wake me up in two hours before closing my eyes.

After taking a much-needed nap, I walked out of the room, searching for Ron. He was no longer on the sofa, so I assumed that he was in his room. I softly knocked on the door a couple of times before turning the knob to see if it was locked, which it wasn't. When I saw that he wasn't there either, I shrugged my shoulders before closing the door behind me. I tried calling him, but his phone kept going straight to voicemail, so I sent him a text. Thirty minutes passed, and I still heard nothing from him, but I knew that I wasn't about to spend my whole day waiting for him to return. Looking out the window, I decided that I was going to head to the beach. I didn't have a swimsuit, but I knew that there was probably a store or a gift shop along the way that I could buy one from. Changing into some more presentable clothes, I left the suite.

It took me a little bit over an hour, but I had finally made it to the beach. I would've been here sooner, but I was terrible with directions. I had stopped at a gift shop that was near the resort that we were staying in and had picked out a little cute blue and black floral two-piece bikini, a cover up, some flip flops, sunscreen, and a big straw bag to keep my clothes in. I asked the woman at the cashier for directions while she rang up my things. After hearing her trying to explain what signs and streets I should look for, I was even more confused, so I just used the GPS on my phone to lead me in the right direction; even then, I still got lost a couple of times.

After changing in a stall, I looked around to see if I could find an empty beach chair amongst the sea of people. Once I spotted one, I jogged to it so no one else would take it. I pulled out the sunscreen that I had purchased and rubbed it on my face, arms, stomach, thighs, and legs. Giving my skin some time to fully absorb the sunscreen before I went to go swim, I looked on as I saw people enjoying themselves. There wasn't a sad face in sight; there were only smiles and laughter. If only I could absorb half of the positive energy these people had surrounding them, then I'd be okay. I was still contemplating on whether I wanted to give up on being an artist or not. Painting would always be my passion. It just didn't seem like it would be my career. *No, Sasha, you will leave those negative thoughts in Texas and enjoy yourself for the remainder of this trip!* I heard my inner voice yelling.

"Aloha," an elderly Hawaiian woman with a smile on her face said to me as she set her chair next to mine. She had a very welcoming and pleasant face, kind of reminding me of my grandma. She wore a bright-pink dress that flowed down her plus-sized body and stopped at her feet. Her hair was in two low pigtails that landed in the middle of her back with two orange flowers on both sides.

"Aloha," I politely replied.

"I see that this is your first time being on this beautiful island." I was taken aback a little, wondering how she knew that. I simple wrote it off as maybe I gave off the vibe as a tourist, so I just nodded my head in response to her.

"You know what I love about my home? It has a loving atmosphere. How people help one another out, not for recognition or praise, but they genuinely care about others. If more people adapted this kind of mindset, then this world would be a better place." I didn't know where this conversation was headed, but I listened on as she continued to talk. "This island has a way of making even your darkest thoughts seem crystal clear."

"What do you mean by that?" I asked curiously.

She looked out to the water for a minute then back at me, still wearing a smile. "I sense a lot of confusion, anger, and sadness flowing through your body. You are at a standstill and not sure how to make your next move. You are unhappy about the current situation that you are in and not sure how to make it better. So I'm here to offer you some light on your situation. Don't stop what you are doing. Keep going. Your hard work will pay off sooner than you think. Someone that you have recently come in contact with has the power to make all your dreams come true and make your fragile heart strong.

"And this person that I'm talking about will not only be your husband but your soulmate as well. But be warned, there will be a time when you want to walk away from him, and in that time, you will be on the verge of losing him. That's when you will find that your souls are truly connected." The look on her face and the tone of her voice was so serious that it had me spooked. Growing up from where I was from, we were always taught never to entertain people that claimed to be fortune tellers or anything of that nature, because it was considered the works of people that practiced in the dark arts, but here I was, sitting here, involuntarily getting my future told to me, and that scared me shitless.

I opened my mouth to ask her if this was a joke, but nothing came out. I heard my name being called, and I looked in the direction of the voice and saw Ron walking toward us. I gathered my things that were beside my chair. "My friend is calling me, but it was nice meeting you," I nervously said to the old woman before I practically ran into Ron's bare chest.

"Damn, slow yo' ass down. You missed a nigga that much that you running to me? I low-key feel special," his cocky ass said, placing his hands over his heart, smiling his signature smile.

Momentarily forgetting what just happened to me, I stood back and admired Ron's entire appearance. His dreads were no longer in the low ponytail he had them in when I last saw him; instead, he had them hanging freely. The only clothing he had on was a pair of red swim trucks, giving me a view of his amazing body that I had only fantasized about seeing. If I had to describe his body, I would compare it to a football player and not the bulky ones. I was talking about the ones with the bulging muscles and the six-packs. I would've laughed if I wasn't so spooked out. I turned back to look in the direction that I had just left, and the elderly woman was gone. My eyes searched the beach, trying to see if I could spot her location again. I refused to believe that I was hallucinating or seeing some type of spirit.

"What are you looking around for?"

I turned my attention back to him. I wasn't about to tell him what that old lady told me and have him thinking that I was crazy. "Nothing. Why didn't you tell me that you had left? I called your phone and sent you at least three texts, and you didn't respond to either one of them. You do realize that this is my first time being here, and I don't know where anything is at. You just can't be leaving me. I got lost five times just trying to find this place," I whined, crossing my arms.

"Sorry about that. I had some shit I needed to handle real quick, so I couldn't answer the phone. I didn't expect to be gone as long as I was. When I went back to the suite and saw that you weren't there, I opened that text message you had sent, and that's why I'm here now," he explained. "Do you want to go surfing?"

"I don't know how to surf."

"I'll teach you. It's real easy once you get the hang of it."

"Sure, why not?" I asked, agreeing. This could be a fun experience, and I was always down to learn something new. We walked to a surfboard retail shop that was located on the beach. Once we had gotten them, we went straight into the water.

It started off rocky at first, with me falling off the board every time I tried to stand up, and once the waves start coming in, I was completely over learning how to surf, but Ron insisted that I kept going, and after him threatening to leave me stuck in the middle of the ocean, I gave it another try.

"Look!" I screamed in excitement. "I'm doing it! I'm surfing!" I was balancing myself on the board, riding a low wave. My eyes focused on the waves. Briefly, I looked up and made eye contact with Ron, who was sitting on his board while it floated. He looked at me with a huge smile across his face. I could tell that he was pleased that I finally got the hang of it. I was so busy looking at him that I lost my balance and fell off.

I swam my way back to the top of the water, gasping for air. "Are you straight?" Ron asked me. I nodded my head and attempted to get back on the board. "Damn. Your titties might be little, but they look nice as fuck," Ron said, lustfully eyeing me.

I looked at him in confusion. "What are you talking about?" I asked him, but he just pointed to my chest. I looked down and screamed with embarrassment, placing my hands over my boobs. My swim top no longer covered my chest but was floating right next to me. Quickly, I grabbed the top, tying it back around my chest, looking around to make sure that no one around us saw it. I was sure that if I were a couple of shades lighter, my face would've been beet red.

"You could've kept that top off for a little while longer. I was enjoying the view," he said, licking his lips.

"I hope you took a mental picture of them because it will be the last time you see them, pervert," I said, splashing some water in his direction before paddling off.

We stayed in the water for two more hours before deciding to leave. This was the most fun that I'd had in a while. I couldn't remember the last time that I was so carefree, and it seemed that Ron was enjoying himself as well. My skin resembled a prune since we had been in the water for a long period of time, and I was scared to see what my hair looked like.

***

"Hurry your slow ass up before we are late!" Ron yelled, banging on the door while I was putting the finishing touches on my outfit. Since we were leaving tomorrow, he thought it would be a good idea if we went to a luau so I could have the full experience of Hawaii. I wasn't complaining either. "Sasha, I'm giving you five minutes before I leave you here!"

Once I felt like my look was complete, I opened the door with my hands in the air, doing a slow spin so he could get the full view. I thought since we were going to a luau, I would dress for the occasion. I Googled some ideas, and I thought this look would be perfect. I wore a coconut bra that I purchased earlier that exposed my stomach and a grass skirt that stopped a little bit above my knees. I did my hair in some medium-sized twists and put a pink flower on the side. I usually wouldn't dress like this, but I wanted to live a little. After all, I was in a place people considered paradise. "So, what do you think?" I asked, observing his face, awaiting his response.

"I don't know what the fuck you was inhaling while you was in that room, but you got me fucked up if you think you are going somewhere with me wearing that. Take that shit off and put on some goddamn clothes," he spoke calmly, puffing on the blunt he had in his mouth.

"What's wrong with what I have on? I'm pretty sure it will be a lot of woman dressed like this tonight." I huffed, crossing my arms over my chest.

"I don't care how other women will be dressed. That's on them, but I know how you will be dressed, and it sure as hell won't be in that thot ass shit you wearing now. So for the last time, go in that room, and take that shit off before I do it for you, and I promise that you wouldn't want that," he said in a cold tone, still smoking on his blunt. I was about to open my mouth to tell him where he could go, but when I saw the deadly look he had in his eyes, I quickly closed it.

"Well, I don't have anything else to wear," I said with an attitude with my hands on my hips.

"You are really starting to fuck up my high right now." He put out the rest of his blunt and walked out the door. I took a seat on the sofa, crossing my legs in front of me. I grabbed my pencil and pad that I had left on the table and started on a portrait that I'd been working on since last night.

I got so caught up in drawing that I didn't hear Ron come back in the room until he snatched my drawing pad out of my hands, looking at my portrait. I tried getting it back, but my five-foot-seven frame wasn't a match for his six five.

"Aye, is this supposed to be me?" he asked after I finally gave up on getting it back from him.

"Yeah, it was supposed to be my gift to you for bringing me here with you. My previous idea was to buy you something, but I didn't know what you would like, so I thought this would be a good substitute instead," I explained. "I thought it would be more heartfelt, but if you don't like it, I can always get you something else, I guess." I planned on giving this to him when we made it back home to show my appreciation.

"This shit is dope. I ain't never had somebody draw me, and the shit look so realistic," he said while tracing over the drawing with his eyes, looking on in amusement.

While we were on the beach yesterday, I had grabbed my phone and snuck a picture of him when he wasn't looking, and I used that as my inspiration. I rarely drew portraits, not that I didn't like doing it. It was just that I preferred to freestyle with my art where I didn't have to be as tedious.

"Thank you. I'm happy that you like it. What's in that bag you are holding?"

He removed his gaze from the drawing pad and looked down at the bag he held in his hands before throwing it in my direction. "What's this for?" I asked, opening the bag and pulling out what looked like a blue dress with small flowers design.

"It's for you to wear tonight because I sure as hell wasn't about to let you wear that shit you picked out." He sat down on the sofa before looking back at me. "What are you waiting on? Get dressed so we can go. Shit, I'm hungry." And just like I predicted, his asshole side had resurfaced, and it only took a day and a half.

Once I got dressed, we headed out to the place that held the luau. When we arrived, I was in awe. I was like a kid that attended the circus for the first time. Everything I saw had me hyped from the men that were doing tricks with fire sticks to the women shaking their hips in their grass skirts. I got distracted so many times that Ron had to literally grab my hand and pull me to our table that was located in the middle section. The host announced that the show was taking a brief intermission, and then it would resume shortly. We ordered our drinks, and Ron ordered the food because I couldn't make up my mind on what I wanted.

"So Sasha, tell me. What do you want out of life?" Ron asked me while I was sipping on my fruity drink. I was a little taken aback by what he asked; not that it was a bizarre question or anything like that, but I just didn't expect him to care about my life like that since he didn't show any amount of interest in me.

I swallowed the rest of my drink before I cleared my throat to speak. "I honestly don't know, because I'm still trying to figure that out myself. If you are talking about career wise, then of course, I want to be successful. I mean, who doesn't? I want to be recognized for my work as an artist and hopefully my name become mentioned with the greats, but I also want the consumers to not feel cheated in any type of way. Like, you know how when people reach a certain level of success or money, they just start putting out anything because they know that it will sell? I never want to get to that point where money ruins my moral. And if we're talking about the general goal of what I want out of life, I would say just to be completely and fully happy. I want the career, the family, and the kids with the big house and white picket fence and a cat because I really don't care for dogs. I know that sounds like a cliché, but it's how I feel. So what about you? What do you want out of life?"

"I already got what I want out of life. I'm my own boss, my businesses are doing good, and I got more money than I know what to do with. I get to travel around the world whenever I feel like it and have lived in other countries. What more could I ask for?"

"How long are you planning on staying in the line of business that you are currently in?" I asked, referring to the drug game.

"Not for long. I already got my exit plan in motion. I'm giving myself another three years of this shit, then I'm officially out. I can't see myself doing this shit forever. It's too many cons. I'm not trying to spend the rest of my life looking over my shoulder, wondering if or when I'mma get popped. That shit is for the birds."

"What about love and a family? Do you plan on having one of your own, or are you planning on being a male hoe all your life?" I half joked.

He rubbed his chin, staring at me with those sexy hazel eyes of his. "A male hoe, huh?" He smiled. "I wouldn't consider myself a 'male hoe.' I'm just a single male that happens to enjoy having sex with several different women, but to answer your question, I really don't have any thoughts of having a family or that love shit. I have seen too much fucked up shit that women do when they are in their feelings about some shit to even trust one. You can say I have a bit of a trust issue problem, but if I do find a woman that I can see myself trusting 100 percent, then I would definitely want a family, but I highly doubt that would happen any time soon, so I'mma continue doing me."

I felt my heart sink after his confession. Here I was, catching feelings for someone who just admitted to not only having sex with multiple women, but he didn't even believe in being in a relationship. At this point, I just wanted to be as far away from him as possible; not because he did anything wrong, but I didn't know how long it would be before my facial expression showed how I felt on the inside.

"Are you good? Why you suddenly look like you about to cry or something?" he questioned with a hint of concern in his voice. I guessed my cover was blown.

"Yeah, I'm good. I was just thinking about something. That's all." I gave him a forced smile.

He looked like he didn't believe me, but he didn't push the issue. For the rest of the dinner, we watched the show in silence. He tried to make conversation once or twice, but after he saw that I was giving him short answers, he eventually got irritated and stopped.

Once we made it to our suite, we went our separate ways. I pulled off my dress and headed into the bathroom to take a quick shower before I went to bed. I stood in the shower, thinking back to the conversation at dinner. *Maybe I did overreact. I mean, just because he said that he didn't see himself being in a relationship right now didn't mean I had to treat him like that. Maybe this was the sign I had been praying for. Maybe we weren't meant to be together. I should apologize to him in the morning,* I thought to myself. After I got out the shower, I lotioned my body up and slipped on some shorts with a tank top and socks. Once my head hit the pillow, it was lights out for me.

*Boom!*

I heard a loud noise coming from outside that woke me up out of my sleep. Rubbing my eyes, I got out the comfort of my bed, walking over to the window. I pulled the curtain back and saw that it was storming outside. As my mother would say, it was raining cats and dogs. The rain was coming down fast and hard. I watched as the strong wind made the trees move from side to side. I started to feel my anxiety surface. My breathing was becoming labored. I hated whenever it stormed. It took me back to the time when I was a little girl.

It was storming one day, and I wanted to play in the rain, but my parents told me that I couldn't. So somehow, I managed to sneak out the back door while they weren't looking and ran outside. It was all good at first. I was running and jumping in puddles, having the time of my life, but all that changed when my foot got stuck in a hole. I tried getting myself out, but it was no use. My foot was in there deep. I called out to my parents, but they couldn't hear me. I lost it when it started thundering and lightning. I saw the lightning hit the ground in our backyard, only missing my body by an inch or two. I screamed to the top of my lungs for my dad while I was sobbing. Eventually, they heard me, and to this day, I had been scared of storms.

Jumping in the bed, I held my pillow close to my body with my eyes closed shut. I tried calming myself down by singing a song to drown out the noise, but once I heard another loud boom, I ran out of my room to the other side of the suite, banging on Ron's door. He came to the door a few seconds later, wearing only a pair of boxers, looking like I had just woke him up out of a good sleep.

"Why are you knocking on my door like that?" he asked, rubbing his eyes with a sleep-laced voice.

I nervously held the pillow to my chest. "I was… I was wondering if I could stay in here with you until the storm passed over. I mean if… if that's okay with you. If it's not, I can just go back to my—Ahhhhh!" I screamed when I heard the loud sound again.

"Come on," he said opening the door, allowing me to enter. He got back in the bed, and I just awkwardly stood there, hugging a pillow, not knowing where I should sit.

"Are you just going to stand there looking stupid, or are you going to come lay in this bed?"

I slowly walked over to the empty side of the bed and got in. I made sure I put a good amount of distance in between Ron's body and mine. Looking up at the ceiling, I tried to calm my nerves, but nothing seemed to work. I looked over in Ron's direction and noticed that his body was turned facing me. I smiled a little as I looked at his sleeping face. I didn't think anyone could look this good while they slept, but he pulled it off. I fought the urge to reach out and trace the outline of his face.

"I know I look good, but you don't have to stare at me that damn hard," he said in a groggy voice, opening him his eyes.

I quickly turned my attention back to the ceiling, embarrassed that he had caught me looking at him while he slept. "What are you talking about? I wasn't staring at you. I was just, umm… looking to see if you were sleep, so don't flatter yourself," I lied. He chuckled before reaching over, wrapping his strong arm around my body, scooting me closer to his. "What are you doing?" I asked.

"What does it look like I'm doing? I moved you closer to me so you can stop doing all that jumping and shit," he replied, looking me dead in the eyes. His gaze was so hypnotizing that I had to break our eye connection. "Since you woke me up out of my sleep, you want to tell me why you shut down on a nigga at dinner tonight?"

My body became stiff. I wasn't expecting him to ask me that, so I didn't know whether I should lie to him or tell the truth. "I don't know what you are talking about. I didn't shut you out. I just didn't have anything else to say." It was half of the truth.

"So you just gon' look me in the eyes and tell me that bold-faced lie? A couple of things you should know about me. I don't like liars, and I know how to read people well. So I'm going to do something that I rarely do and repeat myself, and if you lie to me again, I'm putting yo' ass out and leaving you in there screaming by yourself, okay?"

I started to laugh until I realized that he wasn't joking.

I might as well tell him. It wasn't like I was going to see him anymore after this anyways. I already had it set in my mind that once we touched down in Texas, I was going to avoid him like a plague. I knew I was being childish, but I didn't want to fall for him any more than I already had, only to get my feelings hurt even more. "Since you claim you can read people, then you should have already figured out that I'm feeling you, like a lot. And once you told me that you really can't see yourself in a relationship, I kind of felt like I wasted time crushing on you all these months," I opened up.

"I figured that's what it was. Look, like I told you before. My trust is fucked up when it comes to females, and I don't know if I will ever fully trust one besides my mother." He put his fingers underneath my chin, lifting my head up so I could look him in the eyes. "The reason that I invited you to come with me on this trip was to see if I just wanted to fuck or if it was something more. Don't get me wrong; I still want to see what that pussy's like, but I also want to find out more about you. I'm not going to lie to you and say that I'm ready to be with you, but I do want to see where this could lead if we continue doing what we are doing."

He leaned his face down toward mine, and our lips connected. I felt the same spark that I felt that night we kissed at my apartment. I felt myself becoming wetter with every kiss he blessed my lips with. My body started to have a mind of its own, and I began to slowly grind on his mid-section. I felt his hands roaming all over my body before finding their way into my shorts. I gasped, feeling one of his thick fingers enter my vagina. I tried removing his finger from me, but his hold was too strong. He started going slow, and then he sped up his movement as his mouth made its way to my neck. I felt an overwhelming feeling take over me, and I couldn't hold back any longer, and I came all over his hands. I lay back, trying to catch my breath.

"Don't tell me you are done off that little shit. I'm nowhere near finished with you," he said before throwing the cover from our bodies. I watched on as he slid my shorts off my body, revealing the fact that I didn't have on any panties. "Damn," he whispered with a smile on his face once he saw my neatly shaven pussy. He started trailing kisses up from my legs to my thighs.

I spread my legs open in anticipation of him giving me oral, but to my disappointment, he moved up to my stomach, trailing soft kisses along the way. Ron removed my shirt and threw it on the floor. His mouth covered my small breasts, and I nearly lost it. My hips started to buck, and I was leaking down there. He stopped what he was doing long enough to reach in the nightstand drawer and pull out a condom. I took this chance to see what he was work with in the penis department. My eyes widened when I saw his huge package. Not only was it long, but it was thick as hell. How could something that big fit on a human? Brushing my nervousness aside, I gave him an inquiring look.

"Why you had condoms in your stand? Did you already have plans of sexing me?" I asked with a slight attitude.

He chuckled. "No, but if you stay ready, then you won't need to get ready," he replied, slipping on the condom, getting ready to enter me, but I stopped him, placing my hands on his chest. I had to get something off my chest.

"Before we do this, I think you should know that I'm a... I'm a virgin," I nervously blurted out.

He started to laugh. "You fucking with me, right?" he asked, but once he saw the scared look on my face, he leaned up. "How is that possible? I thought you said that you and ole boy was together for three years or some shit like that, and you mean to tell me he didn't hit that not even once?" Ron got off me and moved to the side of the bed with his hands covering his face, letting out a breath of frustration.

I crawled my naked body over to where he was, placing my hand on his back. "No, we never had sex. The furthest we went was oral sex. Before we got together, I let it be known that I was waiting until I felt like I was ready to have sex, and he told me that he understood and that he was willing to wait for however long because he felt like I was worth it, but I guess after a few years of being with me, and I still didn't give him none, he couldn't wait any longer. I kept hearing a lot of rumors about him sleeping around with different girls, but he always denied it, and I never had any proof, so I believed him until one day I finally saw it with my own eyes."

He turned around to look at me. "Why me, huh? Why do you feel like you are ready now? You been with a nigga for three years, and you didn't give him shit, but we have only known each other for what—six months—and now you feel like I'm the one? That don't make sense to me. I'm not the type of nigga that you want to give your virginity to. I have bitches that go insane once I start fucking with them, and they ass been fucking since their teenage years. I can only imagine how you would be if I were to be your first. I know I'm a fucked-up nigga at times, and I have a certain of level of respect for you to not want to fuck up your life. So that's why I can't fuck you," he said in a sincere voice.

I was trying hard to fight the tears that were threatening to roll down my face. I knew he probably thought he was doing the honorable thing by telling me that he didn't want to be my first, but I couldn't help the hurt feeling of being rejected. Here I was, offering him something special, and he didn't even want it. I moved away from him, grabbing my shorts and tank. I was about to get off the bed, but he grabbed my arm, stopping me.

"You can still stay in here until after the storm is over. I wasn't about to put you out."

I said nothing, only biting my lips to keep from crying. I tried getting up once again, but his hold was too strong on me.

"Look at me," he said, but I couldn't. One, I was still embarrassed, and two, I didn't want him to see my tears that had escaped from my eyes.

"I'm sorry if I put you in an awkward position. I didn't mean to do that. I understand now that you never looked at me in that way, and it's all good." I sniffed a little. "After we make it back home, you won't ever have to worry about me calling or—" My words were cut off by him placing tongue in my mouth.

Ron pushed me on my back and got on top of me with his body towering over mine. He just stared at me with his piercing eyes. I could tell that her was having an internal war within himself. I could feel my heartbeat racing with anticipation, and I waited silently as I wondered what his next move would be.

"I don't want you to leave here and be thinking that I don't have any type of feelings for you, but I know I'm not the type of nigga you need in your life. We can still chill and talk on the phone, but if we fuck right now, I can't promise you that I'm not still going to be doing me, because most likely, I am, but I'll respect you enough not to let my activities come back to your front door. Do you think you can handle that? The decision is yours to make," he said with an expressionless face.

Could I really deal with him being with other women while he dealt with me? The answer was no, but right now, I could give a damn about that. I just wanted to feel like I was his, even if it was for a short period of time. I would deal with the consequences later.

I wiped the remaining tears from my eyes as I nodded my head.

"Are you sure about this?" he asked once more.

Instead of answering him verbally, I pulled his face down to mine, kissing him with as much passion that I could muster up while reaching for his dick and stroking it slowly before placing it at my opening. I really didn't know what to do next, so I was hoping that he picked up where I left off. Catching the hint, he reached between our bodies, rubbing the head of his penis up and down my vagina, causing me to let out a soft moan. Automatically, my hips started to rotate.

"Goddamn, that pussy is leaking for me," Ron said in a whisper. "Are you ready for me?"

"Yes," I desperately said. I tensed up a little when I felt him trying to enter me.

"You good?" he asked with concern. I nodded my head against the pillow. I was nervous as hell, but I couldn't let that show, so I tried to calm my nerves down and relax. In one swift movement, he locked his lips with mine and slowly worked his way into me while making circular strokes of his hips. Once he finally entered me, I fully relaxed my body, wanting to feel him fully.

In the beginning, it was painful. I thought it would feel better after a couple of strokes in, but it didn't. I was starting to second guess everything that Tori told me about sex. This shit did not feel good one bit. As soon as the thought crossed my mind, it quickly left once he sped up the pace. The pain that I felt moments ago had officially turned into pleasure. Moaning a little bit louder than before, I opened my legs wider to allow him to go deeper. I threw my hips back, matching every stroke he gave to me. Getting wetter than I already was, I squeezed my walls around him and sunk my teeth into his neck. He leaned up while still giving me deeps strokes, looking me straight in the face.

When we locked eyes, I could see an emotion that was surfacing in his eyes. I couldn't pinpoint what emotion it was, but as soon as it came, it disappeared. He lifted one of my legs over my head and went even deeper. My eyes closed, and I bit my bottom lip as a tear rolled down my face. I felt an intense pleasure wash all over my body, and my walls gripped his dick as I came. My body lay still, trying to calm down from the high of having an orgasm, but Ron wasn't having that. While still in me, he positioned me on my side and hooked my leg back with his arm and started thrusting harder. I could feel another orgasm on the rise, so I rocked my hips along with his. When I reached my peak, I let out a muffled scream. He covered my mouth, still pounding away. I felt his dick swell inside of me as he released my lips. I looked back at him, and he was biting his lips, and I thought I heard him whisper the word 'shit' before cumming.

Catching his breath, he got out the bed and headed to the bathroom to flush the condom. Feeling the coolness of the room, I pulled the covers over my naked body as I lay back against the pillows.

*OMG, I just had sex for the first time! And it was with Ron,* I thought with a big smile on my face, but it slowly disappeared when I thought of how it would be between us now moving forward.

He walked out of the bathroom, cutting off the lights behind him. Once he made it to the bed, he got under the cover with me, laying his face on my naked chest, careful not to put his dreads in my face. I ran my hands through his dreads, softly massaging his scalp while we lay in silence.

After a while of not talking, I assumed Ron had fallen asleep. I let out a yawn and closed my eyes, preparing to go to sleep.

"Even though we aren't together, you better not fuck no other nigga. That pussy is off limits to anyone but me. If I find out you gave it away, I will body the nigga you fucked, and you'll be dead to me," he said in a groggy voice, but the seriousness in his tone was undeniable. What did I get myself into?

# $\mathcal{S}asha$

$\mathcal{J}$t had been a week since we came back from Hawaii, and for the most part, nothing had changed between Ron and me except for having sex on a constant basis. He would randomly pop up unannounced to my apartment late at night. We would just go at it for hours, and I would later on pay for it at work. I knew that I told him I would be okay with our arrangement, but it was starting to get to me. Every time he left me, or I didn't hear from him, the first thing that popped in my mind was that he was with another girl, giving her what he gave me. I had it so bad that I drove around my apartment complex just to see if I saw his car because I remembered him telling me he messed around with a girl that lived near me. I really needed to get a grip on life.

"A penny for your thought?" Shawn asked, handing me a cup of coffee before taking a seat in front of me, breaking me out of my thoughts.

As promised, today was the day we decided to hang out together. We had already gone bowling and were planning to see a movie later on. Now we were at the Starbucks in the food court at the mall, trying to warm up before we left to go back outside.

"Oh, it's nothing. I was just zoned out." I took a sip out of my cup, not really wanting to talk about it.

"Well, you have been zoned out since I picked you up today. So are you going to tell me what's really going on with you, or do I have to guess for myself?"

"I'm just confused about a situation that I've gotten myself in." I sighed, and my eyes looked around before landing on Shawn, wondering if I should open up to him. He had always been a good listener, and he wasn't judgmental, so I could trust him. "Well, I've been talking to this guy for a while, well, not actually talking but just on a friendly note. It's actually funny how that happened because we couldn't stand each other at first. I thought he was very rude, and he thought I was stuck up. Anyways, when I really started talking to him, he wasn't as bad as I originally thought he was, and I started catching feeling for him even though I knew that he wasn't the ideal type of person to be with. Let's just say he has commitment issues. We had sex, and now it bothers me that he could potentially be with someone else when he's not with me."

Shawn sat in complete silence with a strange look on his face. He leaned back in his chair before speaking. "Did he tell you that he would still be dealing with other women?"

I nodded my head.

"So if you knew all this, then why did you have sex with him?" he questioned.

"Because I wanted to," I whined.

"Okay, so let me get this straight. You had sex with someone that told you he sleeps with other women and that he has trust issues, but you still chose to have sex with him, knowing all this information upfront? Did he pressure you into doing it? Because right now, this story is not making sense to me."

"No, he didn't pressure me. If anything, I was the one to pressure him, but at that moment, I just wanted him to want me, if that makes sense," I sadly responded. Hearing someone else explain my current situation out loud sounded way worse than I thought it was, making me feel even more like a fool.

"I'm going to be honest with you. It wasn't a smart idea to get yourself involved with someone you knew wouldn't take you serious, but you are an intelligent individual, and I have faith that you'll find a solution for this problem. Don't be too hard on yourself. We are still young, so we are going to have fuck ups here and there. Just learn from them and keep it moving," he advised.

I raised an eyebrow. "So what mistakes have you made that you've regretted?" I asked curiously.

"My engagement, for one." He groaned.

"Oh yeah, you never told me the story of why it ended."

He took a deep breath. "Two months before the wedding, I was starting to have doubts about marrying her. Actually, the doubts had been there for a while, but it really got strong around that time. She wasn't doing anything that would have made me doubt her or anything like that. It's just I started feeling like if I married her, I would be making a mistake. So one night, I went by her place so we could talk, and imagine my surprise when I walked in and saw her having sex with not one but two dudes at the same time. Instead of causing a scene, I just walked out the door and never looked back."

My eyes widened with shock. "Oh my gosh. I am so sorry you had to go through that." Walking around the table, I wrapped my arms around him, pulling him into a hug. I felt so bad for him. Shawn was a great person, and he didn't deserve what that bitch did to him. I hugged him for a little while longer before taking my seat again. "So did the heffa try to explain herself to you?"

He shook his head. "No, whenever she saw me, she would put her head down and turn the other way. I guess she was too embarrassed to face me after I caught her. I was hurt for a minute, but then I realized that everything happened for a reason. I prayed to God to show me if I should marry her or not, and the next day is when I caught her."

"What are your feelings about relationships now?" I inquired. "Have you given up on them and became a male whore?" I half joked. Ron's comment had me thinking every man would become one.

He sat in thought for a second. "No. Why would I? Just because it didn't work out for me that particular time doesn't mean it won't work out next time. I'm not about to become something I'm not due to the fact that I got my feelings hurt. That's the cowardly way out. I'm just going to keep being the person that I am, and hopefully, the right woman comes along and appreciates me for that. Who knows? It might be sooner than I think," he said, giving me a longing look.

If I didn't know any better, I would've thought he was hinting at something. Opening my mouth to respond, a voice cut me off.

"Ayo, what's up, cousin? I thought that was you sitting over here," a man said, walking over to Shawn, dapping him up. I didn't know why, but a strange feeling came over me as I looked at the man. I knew I saw him before, but where was the question.

"What's up, Bryan? What are you doing here?" Shawn asked with a smile plastered on his face.

"Just running some errands real quick before I hit the streets again." He turned his attention in my direction and smirked. "Who is this?"

"Oh, my bad. This is my friend Sasha. Sasha, this is my cousin Bryan," he introduced us.

"Have I met you before? I feel like I know you from somewhere," I found myself saying as we shook hands.

"Can't say that we have, but it was nice to meet you. I'll catch up with you later, cousin." He still had the same smirk on his face, walking away from us.

Shawn got up from his seat. "I'm about to use the restroom, and we can leave afterward."

As soon as he left, I pulled out my phone to see if anyone had texted me, specifically Ron. I let out a deep sigh once I didn't see his name on my screen. Clicking out the message, I started playing a game to get my mind off him.

"Excuse me," I heard a woman say to me. I looked up and saw a pretty brown-skinned girl with long, straight hair and a body that could be compared to an Instagram model smiling down at me. She was wearing a pair of jeans that looked as if they were painted on, a black tight shirt, and a blue bombers jacket. Just looking at her had me feeling a little self-conscious.

"Can I help you with something?" I politely asked.

"Actually, you can." The smile she was wearing moments ago had now vanished. "You can stay away from my man."

My face formed into a tight frown. Who the hell was this girl, and what was she talking about. Maybe this was one of Kendrick's hoes. "And who might your man be?" I crossed my hands over my chest with an attitude.

"Ron," she replied, wearing a smirk.

It felt like the wind had been knocked out of me. This nigga fed me a whole bunch of bullshit, talking about how he didn't want a relationship, but had a whole damn girlfriend. I guess she could tell that I was surprised by her revelation because she kept talking. "Oh, you didn't know that he is my nigga?" She laughed. "Let me put you on game. Whatever you thought y'all had was a lie. I've been his girl for close to a year, and even though I know that he steps out on me, he makes it up to me by dropping a band in my lap whenever I need money. Let me ask you something. Have you ever been to his house? You don't even have to respond to that, because I know you haven't. That's *our* home together, and I know that he would never disrespect me like that."

Even though I was hurt beyond words, I wasn't about to give this bitch the satisfaction of knowing that she got to me, so I quietly sat there with my resting bitch face on as she continued to run her mouth.

"I hope you enjoyed the little time that you spent with him. I'm pretty sure he getting bored with you anyways. It won't be long before he tosses you out like the trash you are."

Just as I was about to get up and slap the shit out of this fake bodied bitch, Shawn approached the table, wearing a smile. It slowly faded when he picked up on the tension between this trick and me.

"What's going on, Sasha?" he questioned, looking back and forth between us, confusion evident on his handsome face.

I got up from my seat and grabbed his hands. "Oh, nothing. This fake ass video extra wanted to know if I knew of any strip clubs that were hiring." I looked at her with a fake smile. "I'm sorry, I don't, but I do know a couple of pimps if you are interested." Pulling Shawn by his hand, I stormed out of the mall as this trick stood there watching us.

Once we got in the car, I tried everything to calm myself down, but nothing was working. I wanted to cry, but I refused to shed another tear over that lying ass nigga. A whole damn girlfriend that he lived with? How in the fuck could I have ever been so damn stupid? He told me what type of dude he was from the beginning, and my dumb ass chose to see the good him. Well, I hoped he and that bitch had a nice life together, because I wanted no parts of him anymore.

"Are you going to tell me what that was back there?" Shawn asked, pulling out of the parking lot.

"Remember when you said that if you pray for something, God will answer?"

He nodded his head.

"Let's just say I finally got the answer I've been asking for. But enough about that. We are going to enjoy the rest of our day together." I forced a smile on my face. I hoped I sounded more convincing than I actually felt.

He looked at me with a raised eyebrow before saying, "Okay."

*Fuck Ron and everything he stands for. I hope his dick falls off when he fucks that bitch* was my last thought before I pushed him to the back of my mind and enjoyed the rest of my time with Shawn.

#  Ron

"The numbers have been coming back looking good, and the plug that my dad put us on has been making us a killing!" Justin exclaimed excitedly, rubbing his hands together with a smile on his face.

"Yo' block-headed ass should've been asked your dad to hook us up. We could've been making triple the money we've been making," Bryan said, taking a big gulp of his beer.

"Nigga, fuck you!" Justin spat.

I watched on as both of these niggas went back and forth with each other. We were at Justin's house, playing a game of Spades as we went over business. We were in the middle of a discussion on how the numbers were looking for the month, and everything was running smoothly ever since I got rid of that nigga a couple of months ago.

Getting bored with listening to these niggas clown each other, I picked my phone up and shot Sasha a text. I hadn't heard from her in about two weeks now, and that shit was starting to piss me off. Every time I called her phone, it went straight to voicemail, and when I went to her crib, she didn't answer the door. I was starting to think something had to be wrong with her until I was pulling up to Bria's apartment and saw her leaving out.

I was tempted to follow her little ass, but I had to remember who the fuck I was. What I looked like chasing behind a female when I had a million others that would be happy for me even to speak to them? I wasn't gon' lie; it was low-key bothering me that she had been ignoring my ass. I didn't want to admit it, but I was feeling something strong for her, and I didn't know exactly what it was just yet, and I was trying to figure it out. I thought if I fucked her, then it would go away. Instead, it made whatever I was feeling even stronger.

*Me: I'm pulling up on you later on tonight. We got some shit we need to discuss.*

Stuffing my phone back into my pocket, I directed my focus back on the game.

"Are y'all niggas going to keep arguing like a bunch of bitches, or are we going to finish this game? If not, I can leave." I was already agitated that Sasha had been dodging me. Now I had to put up with these niggas arguing every five seconds over stupid shit.

They both exchanged looks before looking at me. "Nigga, are you on your period or something? You've been hostile as hell for the past couple of weeks. If you need some pads and a Tylenol, I can go upstairs and get you some. I know Tori got it in our bedroom somewhere." They both broke out into a fit of laughter.

I wanted to curse them both out, but I was sure their stupid asses would've turned it into another joke, so instead of acknowledging what Justin said, I stuck up my middle figure.

"Oh shit. Speaking of your girl, I know what I've been meaning to tell y'all, but it kept slipping my mind," Bryan said, getting both of our attention.

"What the fuck you mean, speaking of my girl? Did you see some shit? Was she with another nigga?" Justin mean mugged Bryan.

"Calm your wild ass down. This ain't got shit to do with her. It's about her cousin," Bryan replied, and my ears perked up at what he had to say about Sasha. "Anyways, I was at the mall, and I notice my cousin at the food court with somebody. I walked over to him to speak, and when I looked at the chick, I saw that it was that Sasha girl. Since it looked like they were on a date, I spoke and left." Bryan cut his eyes at me, trying to see if I would have a reaction. Even though I was fuming on the inside, I played it cool, making it seem like I was bothered.

"Are you sure it was a date?" Justin asked him. "They could've just been old friends are something."

I had a couple of conversations with Justin about Sasha, so he knew that she just wasn't just a girl that I fucked on.

"Yeah, they were laughing and talking, looking real cozy and shit," he egged on. "At one point, I saw her even hugging him."

I got up from my chair and stormed to the door. I didn't know what the fuck she thought this was. That was probably the reason her ass had been dodging me and shit for the last two weeks. If she thought I was playing about killing a nigga that even got close to her, then she was surely mistaking. I was about to show her I wasn't the motherfucker to play with.

"Aye. Don't do anything stupid, nigga. I don't have time to be bailing your ass out of jail over no dumb shit!" Justin called out to me before I slammed the door.

I was headed straight to her apartment until I realized that she taught her art class every Saturday around this time. I made an illegal U-turn at a red light and sped off to the community center like a bat out of hell.

Once I made it to my destination, I hopped out of my whip and stormed into the place. I peeked my head inside every room until I finally located her. I stood in the doorway, watching her go around the room, helping her students. Her face lit up every time a student did a drawing right. I was so caught up with staring at her beautiful face that I had forgot why I came here in the first place.

I knocked on the door, instantly getting her attention. Once she saw it was me, she rolled her eyes and walked over, plastering a fake ass smile on her face. "May I help you with anything?" she asked, trying to hide the attitude I could clearly see she had.

"Actually, you can. Come outside with me real quick so I can holla at you," I said through gritted teeth so she knew I wasn't playing with her.

"Hey, Ron." My little cousin waved at me. "Do you want to see what I drew?" he asked, raising up his picture.

"Not right now, little man. I have to talk to your teacher real quick, but I'll see it once we get done talking, aight?"

He nodded his head before picking up a paintbrush.

I turned my attention back to Sasha, who looked like she wasn't about to move. Chuckling a little, I peered down at her and spoke in a low tone so only she could hear me. "Don't make me repeat myself. You already know how I feel about that. So either you follow me out this room, or I embarrass your ass in front of the kids. You pick."

Looking defeated, she told the kids to continue what they were doing, and she would be back in a few minutes. She walked out of her room, and I followed behind her. Once we made it outside, I spun her lil' ass around so we were facing each other.

"What the fuck was so important that you had to drag me out of my class? You do realize this is a fucking job," she spat, hugging her body to keep warm from the cold air.

"I'mma need you to check that funky ass attitude of yours and remember who the fuck you are talking to. I guess that nigga that you've been fucking with got you feeling bold and shit," I said, grilling her.

"Nigga? What nigga? You must be confusing me with your lying ass. I met your girlfriend. She's a real lovely person. I see why y'all are together because y'all both are some rude ass people. How could you not tell me that you were in relationship? What's up with that shit you were spitting about having trust issues and how you thought relationships weren't for you? You had me out here looking like a fucking fool! I can't believe that I trusted you enough to give you something so special!" she yelled, trying to fight back her tears.

I looked at her with my brow furrowed in confusion. "What are you talking about? I don't have a damn girlfriend. I told your ass that already. I don't have a reason to lie about no shit as simple as that!" I hissed.

Letting out a laugh, she rolled her eyes up to the sky. "You must think I'm stupid, huh? So that fake ass Bernice Burgos lookalike wasn't your girl? Then tell me why she said that y'all live together and shit?

Tell me why she went out of her way to tell me that she is used to you cheating on her, and in return, you give her money? Explain that!" Sasha said, crying.

As soon as she said that, I immediately knew who she was referring to. "You are talking about Amber's crazy ass. She has never been my girl. She was a bitch that I used to fuck that I cut off because she was crazy as fuck. I would never cuff that delusional ass broad." That girl had one more time to do some stupid shit before I choked the life out of her.

"So you don't have a secret girlfriend you are hiding from me?" she asked in a skeptical voice.

"Fuck no! I don't have time to be dealing with y'all emotional asses right now. Now that we got that settled, who the fuck you went out on a date with a couple of weeks ago?"

She scrunched up her face. "I haven't been on any date."

"Don't lie to me. You know I hate that shit. Who was that nigga you was with at the mall?"

"Mall? What mall—Oh, you are talking about Shawn. He is just a friend from high school."

"High school, huh? You better be telling me the truth. You remember what I told you that night in Hawaii. I wasn't playing when I said that shit."

"Why does it even matter who I be with? It's not like you care about me!" she spat.

"Who said I don't care about you? That's you assuming shit." I started to walk away. I didn't have time to entertain her right now. I got the answer the I came here for.

"I'm not assuming. It's facts. You don't care about me. The only thing you want is my vagina. I can't believe that I allowed myself to fall for someone like you. You are selfish and only care about yourself. Fuck everyone else's feelings."

I turned around and made my way back toward her, giving her a cold stare. "If that's how you feel, then I can't do anything about it! But don't tell me how I motherfucking feel!" I pointed to my chest. "I do care about you, but I know I'm not the nigga that you need in your life right now! I have shit I'm dealing with, and I know I won't be able to give you my full attention! So if you want to walk away from me, then go! I don't know what else you want from me!" I barked back.

"I want you to say that you care about me just as much as I care about you! I want to know that I didn't make a mistake when I chose you. I want you to open up to me about the things going on in your life. I want to be the only woman you have sex with and the only one that matters." Her tears were resurfacing.

I just stood there, peering at her. I wanted to do everything she said, but I knew I couldn't, at least not right now. I could see myself being with Sasha, but I knew that I had a lot of shit that I needed to work on internally, and until that happened, maybe I needed to keep my distance.

After a while of not saying anything, she looked at me with the saddest eyes I'd ever seen. "I fell in love with someone that's not even willing to give it a try. And the sad part is even after everything you told me, I still thought it was a chance that you might. I finally get it now. I'm not the one for you, and you're not the one for me. Goodbye, Ron. It was nice knowing you," she said, standing on her tiptoes, giving my jaw a gentle kiss before running back into the building.

Everything in me wanted to chase behind her and tell her how I really felt about her, but my pride wouldn't let me. My pride had me getting back in my whip, driving off, and not once looking back, in fear that I would be tempted to turn back around.

# Sasha

$\mathcal{I}$ was lying on my couch with all the lights in my house off except the TV screen. I was in the middle of watch *Waiting to Exhale* with a big bowl of chocolate ice-cream and a bag of vanilla cookies. I was watching the scene where Russell had come to Robin's house after being with his wife.

"You don't need him, with his trifling ass!" I yelled at the screen like they could really hear me. I was still in my feelings over Ron, but I was slowly—and I did mean slowly—trying to get over them. It had been three days since he basically told me we couldn't be together, and I walked out of his life. There were times that I wanted to text him, but I fought my urge. It was hard, trying to detox someone out of your system that was not only your first, but y'all had built a friendship as well. After we finished having sex, he would hold me and talk to me until we fell asleep. There had been plenty of times that he spent the night and even bought me breakfast so I wouldn't be hungry at work. It was the little things that made me fall in love with him, not just his sex. I was starting to get to know the real him, but it seemed as if he didn't want that, so it was best I ended whatever we had.

A knock at my door tore my eyes away from the movie. I got up and opened the door. Shawn walked in behind me. "What you got going on over here? I feel like I just walked into a 'no man allowed' zone." He gestured toward the movie and the snacks I was eating.

I moved my blanket off the sofa so he could have somewhere to sit down. "I'm just chilling," I said, patting the cushion beside me.

He took a seat and watched the movie with me. "I just don't understand men. Y'all have these perfectly good women chasing behind y'all, but y'all don't notice them until someone else want them," I vented.

"Don't say y'all, because every man ain't the same, just like every woman not. If I knew I had a good woman chasing after me, it wouldn't be any chasing. She would already be my woman."

I gave him a 'nigga, please' look. "I don't believe that, Shawn. Niggas be all confused about their feelings until they see that woman moving on, trying to be happy with someone else, then all of a sudden, they want to be with her," I replied, rolling my eyes with a cookie in my mouth.

"If a man really wants a woman, he will make it known. The woman wouldn't have to guess how he feels about her. The men you came across weren't really men; they were just boys." He used the same tone he used that day at the mall like there was a message hidden in there for me to decode.

I felt my phone vibrating and saw Tori's name pop up on the screen. She probably didn't want anything but to know what I was doing, so I placed my phone on silent and made a mental note to call her back once Shawn left.

Sitting my phone on the table, we finished watching the rest of the movie in silence. Once it was over, I leaned my head on the back of the pillows and stretched out my arms. I looked at Shawn and noticed that throughout the rest of the movie, he wore a serious expression.

"A penny for your thoughts?" I smiled, using the same words he used on me.

He let out a deep breath before gazing me in the eyes. "I don't know how you are going to react after what I tell you, but I need to get this off my chest. Remember when I told you a couple months before the wedding that I started to have doubts of getting married to her? The reason behind those doubts was you."

My eyes widened in disbelief.

"I have been in love with you since high school. You are the only person that didn't judge me based off my appearance and took the time out to know me. I wanted to tell you since our junior year how I felt, but I never had the courage to do so, fearing that you would reject me. Once we gradated and both moved to different states, I thought I had lost my chance, so I began trying to date. My ex reminded me of you a little. Y'all had the same wild, curly hair, body type, and couldn't dance for shit, but that's where the comparisons stopped. She was a taker, and you are a giver. You are caring and loving even to people that doesn't deserve it. That's one of the reasons I fell in love with you."

I sat there, speechless. Shawn had been my friend for years, and I never even had a clue that he felt this way about me, or maybe there were signs, and I just didn't want to see any. Knowing that I still had feelings for Ron, I didn't know how to respond to him. Maybe if he would've come back before Ron and I became close, then yes, I would've been with Shawn's sexy ass. Sadly, that wasn't the case.

Just when I was about to speak, he planted his lips on mine. My initial reaction was to push him off, but then something came over me, and I closed my eyes and kissed him back. Maybe Shawn was who I really needed, and Ron was just a distraction.

When I finally open my eyes, I notice the screen on my phone lighting up with Tori's name. Breaking our kiss, I grabbed my phone and accepted the call. "Hey what's—"

Before I could finish, she cut me off. "I've been trying to call you for almost an hour! You need to come to the hospital now! Ron has been in an accident!" she yelled through the phone.

As soon as the words left her mouth, everything around me went black.

## TO BE CONTINUED...

Text ROYALTY to 42828 to join our mailing list!

To submit a manuscript for our review, email us at
submissions@royaltypublishinghouse.com

Text RPHCHRISTIAN to 22828 for our
CHRISTIAN ROMANCE novels!

Text RPHROMANCE to 22828 for our
INTERRACIAL ROMANCE novels!

# Get LiT!

Download the LiTeReader app today and enjoy exclusive content, free books, and more

CPSIA information can be obtained
at www.ICGtesting.com
Printed in the USA
LVOW13s1809280218
568199LV00016B/1023/P